I0635887

Ellen and The Hummingtree

No part of this book may be used or reproduced by any means, in whole or in part, or in any manner whatsoever including any form of electronic data retrieval system or manual copying without written consent of the author except in the case of brief quotations embodied in critical articles and reviews.

Contact the author: audrey@persona.ca

Cover Design and Artwork

By Susan Ruby Krupp,

Yuneekpix.com

Copyright Registration #1093004

Austin, Audrey 2nd ed.

ISBN #978-19266146-7-0

ELLEN and The HUMMINGTREE

a novel

written by Audrey Austin

Cover Design and Illustrations throughout

by Susan Ruby K. – Yuneekpix.com

A strong woman of faith,

Ellen sits beneath her Hummingtree

and talks to God through the yellow quartz rock.

She gifts us with glimpses of her life
and shares the import of her personal relationship
with family, friends and with God.

She allows us to witness her vulnerability
and invites us into her heart
where we experience her joys and sorrows.

In a few instances the author has drawn from her
life's experience but, in essence, Ellen is a composite
of many beautiful, spiritual women the author has
known and loved throughout her journey.

It is hoped you will welcome Ellen into your heart
and it is hoped you will enjoy the stories she shares
with you in this book; her fictional, magical, mystical
memoirs
titled <u>Ellen and The Hummingtree</u>.

At the outset of this writing journey we met.
I became acquainted with her
and now I can say that I truly like Ellen.
She has the courage of her convictions
And no matter what life threw at her,
she never lost faith.

Audrey Austin, Author

Dedication

This work of fiction is dedicated to my dear sister, Eleanor, whose loving support has encouraged me to stick with it and complete the writing of <u>Ellen and The Hummingtree</u>. I am inspired by my sister's deep convictions and her strong faith in God. In telling Ellen's story I have attempted to instill these attributes into the very fiber of the main character's being. It is my pleasure to dedicate this book, with love, to Eleanor Lambert.

Contents:

ONE

ONE:

Ellen's Hummingtree:

I swear sometimes it feels like all the testy trauma tore up my life just yesterday but it has, in fact, been many long and eventful years since my marriage stopped cold in its tracks and ended in that dirty word called divorce. Although I've been a single woman for a very long time there are some people in town who still call me Mrs. Dawson; that is if they bother to call me at all. I've noticed that the older I get the less often the telephone rings.

I know divorce is as common as a cold today and sometimes I think it is just as contagious but back then when Jerry left me alone to raise the girls on my own people couldn't wait to start laying blame.

Yes, I was the unwilling target of nasty neighbourhood gossip. I wish many of the exciting escapades people attributed to my life after Jerry took off did take place. I wish all the gossips who did their best to slander my name by nattering about my so-called romantic adventures had been telling the truth. I wish my life had been as exciting as everyone else seemed to think it was or imagined it should be.

But I can't wish and waste my life away. It seems that some people are never at a loss to have something controversial to say about me and whether they know what they are talking about or not doesn't seem to enter the equation or influence their decision to keep that motor-mouth wagging. Gossipy rumor mongers! The town is alive with them!

I don't have a lot of time for blame-laying. And even if I did I wouldn't have the slightest idea where to start. Fault-finding is an excursion I will leave to my neighbours who seem to find great pleasure in the exercise.

Sure, I could blame Hollywood for creating the illusion that divorced women are always conniving, manipulating and doing their best to steal another woman's man. I could blame Jerry for leaving me in such a predicament at a time when divorce was not yet a socially acceptable rite. I could blame the people who, prior to the divorce, pretended to be my staunch allies and faithful friends for not wasting any time in changing the tune they were singing once I was left alone to raise my children.

I could blame myself for letting the opinions of others get to me but as days turned to weeks, to months and to years, it didn't take me long to learn that there was really no point in blaming anyone. The challenge was to accept. That challenge remains today but I do my best to deal with it one precious day at a time.

Once my marriage ended I knew that I simply needed to move on with my life. I needed to get past the nastiness that tried to hold me back. Regardless of my efforts it remained true that, no matter how challenging and difficult my very existence became once Jerry left; people still had this glamorous idea carved into their minds about the gay divorcee.

It may be hard to believe but it was very true that in those dismal, dire days female friends said to me that if they were going to come by for a visit they would need to come alone. They had the nerve to tell me that they no longer wanted to visit me with husbands in tow. It is equally true that these same so-called married female friends no longer included me in their invitation lists for dinners, shows or monthly card parties. I was ostracized to the point that I am surprised one of my judges didn't create a sign that I could wear around my neck declaring to the world that I am a dangerous felon out to steal the husband of any woman dumb enough to bring him into my realm.

Although they believed it themselves, I know I wasn't being ignored by these women for the reason that they didn't trust me. I do know it was because they didn't trust their own husbands and rightly so. If those husbands had been mine, and thank God they were not, I wouldn't have trusted them either. No less than six of these faithful, loving men came knocking at my door not so very long after word got around that Jerry doesn't live here anymore.

No, I did not invite one of these errant husbands into my home but, regardless, it is true that my divorce did raise more than a few eyebrows.

My name is Ellen Dawson. People who know me well call me Ellen but these days these well-meaning folks are few and far between because experience has taught me well. Today I know how to keep my distance. I know the bountiful benefits of boundaries. I've learned over the years that it doesn't always pay to let people get too close.

Most people in this town don't know me at all but they delight in the scandal found frolicking in their imaginations. Rumors multiply faster than rabbits. Gossip bites are worse than those from black flies. Sometimes you just can't see them coming. Hearsay passes from one gossip's mouth to another's ear and so it goes over and over again. Yes, back fence prattle abounds in this small northern town but for the most part I just keep my eyes open and my ears shut tight.

I know that there are some who call me plain crazy.

Of course, after all that has happened, there are some who don't call me at all like they used to. I'm not going to tell you that being ostracized and being called crazy doesn't bother me. The truth is that it upsets me quite a lot but these feelings are something that I keep safely tucked away as my own little secret; one that, until now, I have shared with no one. I have no intention of giving people the satisfaction of knowing they have injured my pride or hurt my feelings. I pretend that the judgment of others means nothing to me. Just like water off a duck's back! Yes, that's what I would say if anyone ever took the time to ask.

Yes, I have learned to keep things to myself. Sometimes I feel full to bursting but keeping it all in is something at which I have become well-practiced. It's only because I am growing older that I am feeling this necessary need to write things down. Putting everything else aside, I truly believe in my heart that it is important to tell my story about the yellow quartz rock that lives constant beneath my Hummingtree. And I believe it is important that I tell my story while I'm still able to share it; before I grow too old to remember the details.

Some days I hate to admit my age and other days I feel proud of the fact that I am growing old. I believe the very fact of aging is an achievement given that we live in an unpredictable and ever changing world.

Since I've never felt free to talk openly about my life, I hope I will find my way to continue to write things down; to tell my story. I want to do it justice and, in order to do so, I have to prod and sometimes push my thoughts way down deep into my overflowing but sometimes stopped up memory bank because, in truth, it all started fifty-six years ago. That is when I first discovered the huge, yellow quartz rock in the back yard. On that long ago day I had no idea where the rock had come from. It just appeared out of nowhere.

Now I know you are thinking that is plain impossible. A huge, indeed, a massive rock does not just appear out of nowhere.

And, of course, you are correct! Nevertheless my large yellow quartz rock did exactly that.

In my backyard it just appeared out of nowhere one day long ago. No one was more surprised than me to see it at the time. I wasn't looking for this crazy kind of experience or wishing for things to happen the way they did. I was an ordinary pre-teen who didn't think too far beyond saddle shoes and rock and roll.

There is no room for retrospect to find and make a home in a young child's mind. Borrowing a quotation from the King James Bible I now know that, *"All things are possible to those who believe."* But I didn't know that back then.

With closer inspection on the day that I discovered my yellow quartz rock I could see that there was, indeed, a hole in it. Yes, it was a tiny opening but I could see it clearly. My eyes are dim these days and I probably wouldn't even be able to see that hole today if I didn't already know it was there but in those days my eyes were sharp and sensitive to everything around me. I found it strange that this tiny hole located near the centre at the top of the huge rock snaked its way deep down beneath the otherwise smooth and unmarked surface. I was a naïve but very curious young girl that wondrous day of discovery. It was a natural reaction for me to lean over the rock. I did so and I rested my ear against that opening.

The older I get the more my memory is a clown that teases and plays tricks on me. I do my best to focus but my memory often seems to have a mind of its own. Even now as I write, although it's my intention to tell you more about the day I discovered my precious quartz rock, my memory wants to take me on a variety of side-trips. These trips take me to places; always places in the past whether I am in a travelling mood or not.

And now this foolish old woman is suddenly a young girl on her way to school. I see myself walking arm in arm with friends throughout the city streets. I see myself as a student roaming the high school hallways. I am on my way to class. I'm dressed much the same way as my best girlfriends. I'm wearing a colourful, stylish neckerchief tied around my neck, a white, sleeveless blouse, and two white stiffly starched crinolines that crackle with every step I take beneath my Elvis Presley skirt.

But there are two things that stand out in my mind more than anything else when I remember those years. These two things are the discovery of my Hummingtree which I am going to tell you about soon and the ownership of my precious white and navy saddle shoes.

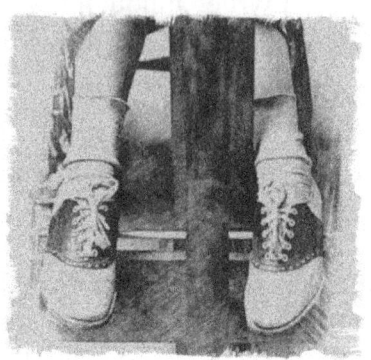

Saddle shoes were worn by all the kids in high school. The only time we took them off was to attend the Friday afternoon sock hops where we danced in the high school gymnasium to *Bee Bop a Lula* and *Blueberry Hill* or when we attended gym classes wearing our one piece blue bloomers and white running shoes.

Those saddle shoes took me back and forth to school; to the Friday night double feature at either the local movie theatre or at the drive-in theatre if I was lucky enough to land a car date that weekend. The only time I did not wear my saddle shoes was on a Sunday morning when my mother insisted I attend Sunday morning worship service at the local Methodist Church. On those mornings I would wear my pumps with the two inch heel. I also wore short white gloves, and a tiny fitted hat with a veil. We would walk to church and I remember wearing my favourite shorty coat. I owned three pairs of pumps and I would wear either white, beige or black depending upon the time of year.

But saddle shoes were my absolute favourite and I am very surprised this fashion has not been revived since the fabulous fifties; a time when I danced in the living-room with my friends listening to the music on American Bandstand hosted by Dick Clark; a time when I walked to school wearing those saddle shoes carrying my school binder in both arms held tightly against my chest. It was just what every teenaged girl did in those days. I was just like everyone else. I didn't really begin to change until after the day I first discovered my Hummingtree.

I enjoy the memories of those long ago days. It seems to me now that I am growing older that I remember my childhood years better than I can remember what I had for breakfast this morning.

Although it happened long ago, in my mind it feels just like yesterday when I was twelve years old and out at the lake with friends. No longer wearing my saddle shoes, pedal pushers and cute little summer top, I was barefoot and wearing a pretty one-piece blue swimsuit. I was never a good swimmer and while the other kids jumped in I was the hesitant observer standing there on that long wooden dock. Full of beans they were and, when I least expected it; some playful boys ran up behind me and pushed me off the dock. I delved into the Lake Simcoe depths. As luck would have it, the strap broke on my bathing suit just before I plunged into the water. By the time I came back up for air I was spluttering. Worse than that, my newly burgeoning breasts bobbed like pink baby balloons atop the pristine water. Trying to tread water and hold my bathing suit up at the same time was a fearful challenge for a weak swimmer such as me. Yes, I live to tell the tale but that day I can assure you I wished I could die. Yes, I truly wished I could die.

And then more than twenty years later I can never forget the gnawing, persistent pain I felt when Jerry left me. In my view the death of a relationship cuts deeper than the death of a loved one. When a beloved dies, a memorial service or a funeral will most likely take place. Friends will bring cards, casseroles and caring thoughts to the one who is bereft. When a relationship dies friends don't know what to do; whose side to take. No one brings food, faith or favour to the doorstep of the bereft. If they visit at all, they bring questions, criticism and, most often, nothing at all.

Later I will tell you more about that stormy night when Jerry left me alone. For now I will share that I, feeling alone, heartbroken and abandoned, lay sobbing on the bathroom floor. I wanted to die.

Yes, I truly wanted to die.

Now here I am in my older age and not so very long ago the doctor told me I would need to use a puffer each morning in order to breathe. I remember my daddy had used a puffer and he died anyway. The day the doctor gives me this news I am already older than my father had been on his day of dying. Because I have to use a puffer I think for sure I will soon die. Yes, I truly think I will soon die.

Throughout my life there have been times when I wished I could die; times when I wanted to die and times when I thought that for certain I would die!

But I'm stubborn and I don't.

I am a survivor!

Today all these penetrating thoughts about death intrude; the wishing, the wanting and the absolute knowing. These thoughts are enticing. They invite me to stay and visit with them. These thoughts tempt me to linger. They do their best to get in the way of the telling but I will persist because, make no mistake, I'm still here to tell my story.

I'm old but I'm not ancient yet. In spite of the cataracts that cloud my vision, when I look at my face in the magnifying mirror that sits on my bathroom shelf over the sink I can see that it comprises a myriad of wrinkles. If I can convince myself to take the time in order to focus I can actually see that each one of my wrinkles is more like an artist's ink drawing of a deeply carved, long, winding road. And I believe that each road exists because of its own story to tell and I believe that at the end of each road is another tale waiting to be shared.

Yes, with age, the body bumps and weighted wrinkles have increased. Indeed they have multiplied but I've often thought that, in His wisdom, God's goodness has allowed my optical vision to simultaneously decrease.

Leave it to man to interfere with God's plans by inventing a seven times magnifying mirror!

In any event I know that I had better befriend old age because he is moving in whether I like it or not. The good Lord knows I don't want to be developing any new enemies at this stage of the game.

And now here I am, sidetracked again. Let me get back to my story.

I started collecting stones at an early age and today I am the proud owner of a wonderful, large stone collection. The larger stones are scattered around and about the house in the front and backyard gardens. Those which are the size of my hand or smaller fill the large plastic bowl that sits atop the ornamental elephant in my living-room.

As a shy and often awkward child I somehow thought I could find myself; my true, confident, talented and clever self in the stones. When I held one in my hand I could feel its pulsing surge of power. I loved and continue to love stones and as a child, knowing their power, I could only imagine how much more powerful a rock would be.

Everyone, even a child, knows rocks are greater, more powerful, than stones. I knew that a rock was something I could depend upon. Rocks are hard and solid. A rock would never let me down; never disappoint me the way my daddy did. Rocks don't die.

I am twelve years old the day I find it. Huge! A yellow quartz rock squats on the ground under the plum tree by the garden shed in my backyard. Where it came from, I have no idea. It was not there yesterday, that I know for a fact.

I've just been told the news that my daddy is dead. I don't want to accept the truth. To escape the constant cries and worry wallowing in my mother's hurting house the day my father dies, I run out into the backyard. The moment I discover the big yellow quartz rock my whole world changes. It's almost like God is saying, "Ellen, I need to take your daddy away but in his place I am giving you this big, yellow, magical rock."

Yes, reality chases me out of my mother's house and into the backyard that dreadful day. My intention is to climb the plum tree and stretch out under its sheltering branches on the roof of my daddy's shed. On this day I think I will especially like it because I can absorb the energy and the many memories that the roof still holds of the man who had spent so many hours raising the angora rabbits beneath its good, shingled protection.

But when I spot the huge quartz rock at the foot of the plum tree I forget about climbing. Instead I sit down on the ground beneath the tree. I lean against the rock and that's when I discover the tiny hole. Though to this day I don't know what possesses me to do so, I stand up, lean over and hold my ear to the little hole in the rock. Somehow this just seems like the right thing to do.

And I do hear it. I am not imagining the humming sound that escapes through that tiny opening and climbs up the tree's stump into its leaves. I listen and in no time at all, the entire tree is humming. It's magical. Once the hole empties itself of the constant, consistent hum the voice within the rock begins to speak to me. I felt frightened at first but the voice offers me reassurance and a sense of peace within.

"Be still," the soft, sure voice within the rock advises.

I never tell a soul about my discovery of my Hummingtree that long ago day when I was twelve. I knew no one would believe me anyway.

Five years later on my wedding day when I left my mother's home I was overjoyed to discover that my Hummingtree traveled with me. When I moved into my first grown-up apartment I was very surprised to learn that the Hummingtree was no longer a Plum. This time it was an Apple tree.

I'm not quite as surprised the next time I change residence to learn that my Hummingtree is a slim white Birch. At different points throughout my life, no matter how often I moved to a new home, the Hummingtree moved with me. Once it was an Oak tree and another time it was a Maple. Somehow that tree is a lot like me or maybe I should say I am a lot like my

[21]

Hummingtree because we both often changed name and location over the years.

No matter the time or place, my Hummingtree always sheltered the rock; the beautiful yellow quartz rock which speaks to me when there is no one else to overhear. My rock is solid, unchangeable and it constantly abides. If there is anyone within earshot my rock remains silent. My rock is there for me alone.

Throughout my life, as one year turned into another, I learned that my rock is a stronghold. It is here that I can store my deepest thoughts and desires safe from prying eyes and probing nosey-parkers. My rock is always there for me and whenever I feel the need I can sit down and share a conversation with God about what is taking place in my life. I can tell Him how things are going. And the voice of God lives inside the rock and the rock lives beneath the Hummingtree.

Many things changed with time but my rock abides constant and enduring beneath the tree. Today my Hummingtree is a delightful, purple lilac tree. I feel as though the Lilac and I just met yesterday but in fact our first encounter took place nearly ten years ago.

Most people don't believe I'm sixty-eight years of age but on this particular day I am feeling and displaying every minute of it. It has been said that I sometimes appear feeble or tired but appearances are deceiving. Make no mistake; I am strong. My faith keeps me strong. My strength is of the inner variety;

something like the rebar the workers put into the concrete when they are building foundations for houses.

I am strong today because, just like the houses, my life is built on a strong foundation. If I have days when I don't feel as capable as I would like, then I take myself out into the backyard where I sit under the Lilac tree and converse with God through my yellow quartz rock.

I don't do all the talking. The voice within my rock also speaks to me. Together we converse.

I find as I am growing older I am becoming more stubborn and a little less willing to listen to my rock's good advice. Of course I am also becoming just a little hard of hearing. Still there are many more times when I lean over to hold my ear close to the little hole in the rock in order to listen to the shared wisdom.

God is my rock. He has never steered me wrong in spite of myself. I am convinced God, Himself, lives in my rock.

I mentioned this fact to a neighbour one day not so very long ago. The truth is she caught me in the act of listening to His voice. "Ellen, what on earth are you up to?" she asked.

"I'm listening to God, Emma," I tell her. "I'm sure God lives in this rock."

"Ellen, you are a crazy old fool!"

Since that day my neighbour makes a point of not seeing me when I am out in my yard. Oh, she doesn't fool me! I know she just doesn't want to talk to a woman who thinks God lives in a rock. Can't say that I blame her! She can ignore me if she chooses. It's no skin off my nose. I am used to being ignored. I got used to that when I was a just a kid though Mommy never ignored me, at least that was never her intention, but, caught up in the busy-ness of their own lives, everyone else did. I learned how to pretend that I didn't care. So far as my neighbour's rejection is concerned, I pretend it doesn't matter and sometimes the pretense feels more like truth.

Like most old ladies I have many stories to tell. This is the first time I have tried to write anything down but I know I have more than one story to share.

I guess I've already revealed quite a lot about myself but, being a novice, I'm not feeling any strong sense of direction as to exactly how I should proceed in the telling of these stories. I remember my dear mother used to tell me that if I want something done I should simply begin. I guess that's exactly what I'm doing. I am beginning.

Today I am writing. Guess you could say I am giving you a glimpse into my reality. I'm not entirely convinced that, like socks in a drawer, my stories will neatly fold themselves into chapters because sometimes, at my age, I have a tendency to ramble when I talk. Maybe this rambling is a big and possibly even important part of who I am. In any event, I hope through this writing adventure I will be able to provide you with some interesting glimpses into my life.

I don't know who you are. I am optimistic when I talk about you because I am assuming that there will be a *"you"* who will read my words. No, it is a fact that I don't know who you are but by the time you have read my story you will know who I am. And when you know who I am perhaps you will be kind enough to get in touch, if I am still alive, and let me know too because the true identity of the old woman staring back at me in the mirror is something I often question.

I can assure you that my story will not be a linear one because, like a lot of older people, I have a tendency to jump from one topic to another. I've often been criticized for this but, no doubt in spite of the criticism, this bad habit will be displayed throughout my literary journey. Regardless, I promise I will not lose sight of the crux of the matter; my primary reason for wanting to write it all down.

I've told you my name is Ellen Dawson but I haven't told you my full name which is Ellen Angela Dawson. I was born August 12, 1942 to my parents, Leon and Eva MacPherson. I intend to give you more than a glimpse into the lives of my mother and father. They are both in Heaven now and I miss them. I don't have a lot of people to talk to and this is another good reason why I thought I would try my hand at writing things down.

I know there is no escape. I know I'm going to die one day and I don't want to go without ever telling anyone about my Hummingtree and the big, yellow quartz rock through which God speaks to me. In this way I've received comfort and guidance at difficult times when there seemed to be no one else in the entire world to give one fanny's fart about what was happening in my life.

I can't just go to people I know and start talking about the influence my Hummingtree and my rock have had on my life. When I was just a kid I did try that once or twice. I confided in people I thought I could trust. In each case the object of my sharing thought I was crazy.

"Nuttier than a fruitcake!" one said.

"Looney tunes!" said another.

Because I am a sensitive soul, I learned at an early age to keep my deepest thoughts to myself. I like to think I am unique, and in many ways I am, but I have to admit I'm like most people when it comes to being the fodder for other women's need to gossip. I don't like it. One nasty thing said about me is enough to keep me sleepless for a month.

I've made my journey through life as a short person. Being vertically challenged does not bother me in the least except when I'm trying to reach something on the top shelf in the kitchen cupboard. Just thinking about reaching for the top shelf reminds me of my dear cousin, Marielle, but I will tell you much more about my beautiful cousin in greater detail later.

When I was younger my eyes were brighter than they are today. Sometimes I think my poor eyes have seen too much. For sure they have seen much more than they bargained for. Maybe that's why the cataracts are there now; to dim the light that shines on all the bloody horrors happening in this blessed world that seems to be just as tired and worn out as I am.

This week alone I am appalled by despicable sights on the television set. Wars, violence, hunger, and greed are accompanied by frightening revolts by Mother Nature on the evening news. One would think that by now I would have learned to turn the television set off instead of allowing the horror to seep and creep into my ragged thoughts. I'm not so naïve that I don't know that men have been creating these horrid happenings since time immemorial and I'm not so foolish as to think we are living in end times though this time of my life may mark the end for me.

My vision is weak and maybe it's time for my hearing to begin to go too because I am growing tired of hearing about these horrific things including floods, earthquakes, child molestations and murder. It is true that I spent much of my life trying to help others, perhaps without a lot of success. Today I am not even sure that I still like people. But that's okay because I am not sure that people like me either. Maybe that is important and maybe it isn't. I have liked and I have loved. At least once or twice I know I have been loved in return.

I love animals. About this, there is no question in my mind. In my humble opinion animals are kinder and more rational than human beings.

Now I am an old lady but when I was a child I was shy, observant and thoughtful. As a young woman I was slim and trim. I did my best to hide my lack of confidence from others and I don't think anyone ever guessed that I carried an ever-present fear around with me. As a young mother I read Dr. Spock and followed the mothering rules as well as I could. I prided myself on my organizational skills and never for a moment did I consider that I might have control issues. I wanted and adored my children. Though I often, of necessity, was less than generous with material gifts I never gave sparingly of my love and affection.

As a middle-aged woman I juggled family, work, and some sort of a social life, rarely finding the balance I sought. Yes, after recovering from my divorce I did date. The carpenter played a big role in my life; old George did care for me and of Jethro I will give you more than a glimpse or two.

Today, an old woman, I simply wonder how I made it this far; how I survived. But I did and I do.

I was born into a Christian home and since the church carried out all its rituals upon me I guess that makes me a Christian. I've studied other religions though and I am not one hundred percent sure that one is any better than the next. I did go to church some Sundays, mostly at the urging of my cousin Marielle, but the truth is I feel closer to God when I sit under my Hummingtree and talk with Him through my yellow quartz rock.

If God is omnipresent as I was taught when a little girl in Sunday School then God can live inside my rock if He chooses. And who is my neighbour to say he can't? And who is my friend to say I'm crazy?

I am not an uneducated idiot who goes through life making up stories about trees that hum and rocks that talk. I completed a college education. I have skills. My mother always told me I have hidden talents. She was right. They remain well hidden. I can't, with good conscience, say I have any great talents but I must admit I am enjoying writing these thoughts down today. Maybe I will discover that I have a talent for writing. Then again maybe I won't but who's to say I won't?

You may have already gathered that I have very strong opinions on many subjects. For example, I hold a very unrelenting judgment on the subject of abortion. I'm dead against it and I don't mind saying so. Fortunately I've never had to make a personal decision on the matter of abortion. But there was a time when I thought I was expecting a baby and I actually considered doing the unthinkable. Those who know me would be aghast to learn that I considered killing an unborn child. I am aghast at the memory. I'm forever

[29]

grateful that it turned out I wasn't even pregnant at the time.

But my careful thought about having an abortion is just one example of personal drama I could never share with another person. I am, however, able to talk to my rock about my evil thoughts. Even though this near blunder occurred many years ago, I remember the uplifting response I received when I confided in my magical rock.

"There is only one path," the voice in my rock said to me. "You can take as many detours as you choose but there is only one path."

Each time my life takes an unexpected turn I remember that message. I have taken many detours. There is no question about that.

I don't exactly know the reason why but I awoke one morning filled with this urge to write it all down. I want to tell you all about me. Today I have told you about my Hummingtree and my rock. I've lived a long time and I have much more to share. Yet sometimes I think there is nothing more to tell. My tree and my rock are my all.

Why should an old woman suddenly want to write? Who cares what an ordinary run-of-the-mill old woman experienced? Revealing myself in this way will make me vulnerable; susceptible to the judgment of others and if I actually allow others to read my words I will be open to their criticism. This is very frightening yet I am determined to tell my story before I go to meet my Maker. The world will know that Ellen was here.

It's a lovely warm day. I am going out into the backyard now. I'll sit on the bench beneath the Lilac.

Oh, yes, I do believe I forgot to tell you about the bench. For more than fifty years I sat on God's good earth beside the rock beneath my Hummingtree. Just over a year ago the voice within the yellow quartz said to me, "Ellen, my dear, you do not need to continue throughout your journey with a sore, painful, aching back. You are growing old. Get yourself a bench and place it beside me here in the garden."

I did just that. No one shelters and protects me better than my Hummingtree. No one understands me better than my rock. Not even me.

I have written these words. I have introduced myself. I have told you about my Hummingtree and I have told you about my yellow quartz rock. I think it is time now to introduce you to my family. I will begin with an introduction to my grandson, Lucien; a beautiful boy; a boy who has grown up and is now a man with a strong, stable career; one about which a grandmother can be proud to boast. I will tell you how a conversation with God through my rock saved this young boy's life. For this, I am forever grateful.

TWO

TWO:

Under the Hummingtree:

God knows I love my children and with the arrival of my beautiful grandson, Lucien I feel blessed and grateful. I know I'm not supposed to, but if I did play favourites most would probably expect me to pick one of my daughters. But, no, I would not; although they both hold a very special place in my heart. Though I've rarely had the opportunity to voice my feelings on the matter of favourites, if given a chance to talk about such a touchy matter, I would definitely say that my grandson, Lucien, is the kind of boy who melts my heart.

He is a small lad; much smaller than other boys his age and ever since he was a tiny tot he has needed to wear eyeglasses in order to see his way through the mixed-up, grown-up world in which he arrived and found himself living.

Lucien has always seemed to have a tougher time than most with ordinary things that most of us do automatically and without a lot of thought or concentration; simple things like combing his hair, making his bed or tying a shoelace. It's not that he is incapable of learning. He can and he does learn but he is what some would call a slow learner. Sometimes Lucien needs to be shown how to do a particular thing a few times before it registers but once it does he can do it on his own; just not as quickly as others might desire.

As much as I love him, I've always thought he's a bit slow in the head. I've said as much to his mother but she doesn't pay attention to anything I have to say in the best of times.

Lucien's deadbeat dad left my daughter's home when the boy was just five years of age and starting Kindergarten. I know since that day it has been a financial struggle for Carol and I always wished I could be of greater help. Somehow we faced the challenge. We all carried on as best we could. I know it was difficult for my daughter but I'm certain it was especially traumatic for my grandson who was abandoned by his father.

Yes, it is indeed a fact that my Lucien has had more than his fair share of troubles in his short life but there is one day that stands out in my mind over all the others and that is a long ago Tuesday when he was just a little tyke, barely ten years old.

"He's a bit slow in the head," I said again that morning to his mother, my daughter, Carol.

"Learning difficulties, Mom! He has learning difficulties!"

"I know, Carol. Don't you see that's exactly what I'm saying. He's a bit slow in the head but there is no doubt he's a good boy at heart."

[34]

"I give up!" my daughter shouted. Feet glued to the kitchen floor, Carol's anger spat the words at me. "Listen to me, Mom. Once and for all you've got to stop saying that! Lucien has enough trouble getting by at school without you telling him he's a bit slow in the head!"

"I never said any such thing to him, Carol. It's you I'm talking to."

"I've gotta go, Mom, or I'll be late for work. Just watch how you choose your words especially when you are with Lucien and, for heaven sakes, make sure he gets to school on time!"

The slamming back door shook the old kitchen window and reverberated throughout the time-worn walls of my house. Carol was gone before I had a chance to open my mouth; never mind a chance to answer. She just will not discuss the state of Lucien's health and behaviour with me.

And why not? I just do not understand her at all. After all, I am his grandmother and his primary care-giver! Why she thinks she needs to remind me to get Lucien to school on time is beyond my comprehension. Who knows better than Carol that I've been doing it now for more than five years, ever since Peter took off leaving her to raise Lucien on her own?

My son-in-law, Peter, is a loser. As a chartered accountant he earned big bucks but would you believe he paid not a penny of child support for his only son; at least the only one I know about? Carol worked so very

[35]

hard for long hours at her own more paltry job in order to provide for the family while Peter completed his education. It was only because of her willingness to struggle and to give him the opportunity that he was able to get his career off the ground.

As soon as he completed his education and found himself established in a comfortable, stable position in the provincial government office he turned his back on his family and left my daughter in a terrible fix. Deadbeat dad is an appropriate label but I can think of a few more choice words that better describe my feelings about the waste of time my daughter chose to marry. Lucien was only five years old when his good-for-nothing, parasitic dad up and left him without a by-your-leave. Gone! Just like that! Never to return! Worthless bum!

I hate to admit it but it's genetic. Abandonment is genetic. It definitely runs in the family. My dear mother's father stopped supporting his family when my Mom was a young girl. My husband, Jerry, stopped supporting my girls when he was lured away from our home. Jerry had also been abandoned by his father when he was a young boy and now my grandson was growing up without a good father figure in his life.

The sins of the fathers! Negative family patterns are repeating in another generation and so far we have been unable to find the key in order to break the disparaging cycle of abandonment that has always been accompanied by financial struggle. Too often it's a hand-to-mouth, hand-me-down existence when a father's pay cheque is non-existent in a young child's life.

It seems that our family spawns strong, independent and responsible women. But when it comes to the men, with maybe one or two exceptions, the less said the better.

No one knew better than me how tough, and even tragic, life as a single mom can be. It was for this very reason I wanted to help Carol out as much as I could when Jerry left. It wasn't difficult to see that she was struggling to raise my grandson on her own. No woman should ever feel so alone.

At fifty-seven I was doing my best to assist financially but the truth is I barely managed to keep myself afloat on my meager fixed income. As much as I loved my daughter and my grandson I was hesitant to agree when Carol came to me and asked if I would take care of Lucien while she went out to work.

I just didn't feel that I was the best person to look after Lucien and I had my good reasons for feeling that way. My biggest fear was that I might make the mistake of babying him too much in my effort to keep him safe in a world gone mad; a world where bullying was commonplace in the public schools; a world where boys carry guns and girls don't hesitate to use their fists. It was a world very different from the one in which I had raised my children. And it was a frightening, insane world compared to the one in which I grew up many years ago.

Yes, I was hesitant but I couldn't say no. My daughter needed my help. I knew she had no one else to whom she could turn and nowhere else she could safely leave Lucien. I knew she needed to be able to leave her son and go to work with some semblance of peace of mind.

I felt I had no choice. How could I refuse?

Though I had raised my two girls for the most part on my own, I just didn't feel confident about my role in the raising of Lucien. On the one hand there were my daughters who were smart, pretty and popular. Throughout their childhood they were attractive, intelligent girls who just seemed to sail with good grades through the public school system. On the other hand, there was Lucien.

Lucien was a good heart, smart in his own way, yes, but popularity was something that was not part of his daily life's experience. Though he gave the impression he was sincerely doing his best, his grades left everything to be desired. Where my daughters had always looked forward to going to school, Lucien did not want to go at all.

My grandson was unique. It was hard to put my finger on exactly what it was that made Lucien different from other children his age. Innocence swallowed him. Unlike the other kids in the neighbourhood he was not street smart. From the earliest age he was a loner. He didn't seem to know how to give a flip answer to the taunts that came his way. He was always the butt of the joke. He kept to himself and tried to steer clear of trouble but he was an easy target to the other kids. Keeping my eye on him didn't stop the teasing taunts that shadowed him every day on his lonely journey to and from school.

Throughout each week our school day routine never varied. It was fortunate that Carol and I lived in the same neighbourhood; in fact, her home was just a few streets away from mine. Because she had an early start time at her job each morning we all needed to be early risers. Except on weekends, she would drop Lucien off at my house at seven a.m. each morning on her way to work.

Lucien and I would sit at the kitchen table and eat breakfast together. School didn't start until nine a.m. so we had plenty of time each morning to enjoy each other's company. Lucien liked to watch the cartoons on TV after breakfast and this is what he would do while I washed up the breakfast dishes. Lucien thrived on routine. Given my choices I would have preferred a little more spontaneity but I accepted that a strict routine was what my grandson not only wanted but, indeed, also needed. I believe living a more structured life during those times probably taught me much needed lessons in patience and gratitude.

When the weather was good we would sit together outside on the front verandah. Lucien loved sitting on my porch swing or sometimes he would just like to sit on the painted verandah steps. As he grew older he liked to stretch his legs out while he balanced his small body on the top of the verandah's railing. Of course he didn't always want to just sit around doing nothing. Often he would use this time in the morning before school to build amazing things with his Lego. There were even some times when Lucien wanted to help me with weeding or watering the garden.

However he decided to make use of this time, it was always Lucien who would remind me, "Don't want to be late for school, Gram. What time is it now?"

And even though Lucien was the one to remind me of the need for punctuality I noticed he would become irritable as the time passed each morning and it came closer to the time when he would need to leave for school if he was to avoid being late,

I would hear myself saying, "Don't bounce around or you are going to fall off that railing, Lucien." Or I would caution, "If you swing too hard you are going to break my swing!" And there were mornings when I would need to remind him, "Don't be rough on the flowers, son."

Some mornings he wouldn't respond to my warnings at all. And then some mornings he would bounce more, swing harder or deliberately damage a flower.

These mornings I would put my arm around him and ask, "What's wrong, son?"

And he would cry softly and whisper, "I don't want to go to school, Gram."

[40]

"You have to go to school, Lucien."

Most mornings he would accept my decree. And he would ask again, "What time is it, Gram? I don't want to be late."

But there were other mornings when his fear, anger and frustration would sometimes grow out of control. "I'm not going to school today! I am not!" he would yell. If he had been playing with his Lego he would sometimes smash the creation he had been building. Sometimes he would stamp his feet and sometimes he would throw things around; anything that might be within his reach. "I don't want to go to school, Gram!"

I loved this boy but sometimes love just was not enough. On mornings such as these I wanted to be able to say, "Okay, Lucien, stay home with me today. We will work in the garden and go for a nice long walk later on." I wanted to be able to say these things to my grandson. But of course what I did say was, "You have to go to school. Behave yourself now and be a good boy. You have to go to school."

There were many times when I felt that the challenges of raising this boy were too much for me. I wasn't getting any younger and a woman my age doesn't always have the energy or the will to deal with a boy whose mind is filled with fear and torment.

On those mornings, once Lucien was in school, I would go into my backyard and sit on God's

[41]

good earth beneath the branches of my Hummingtree. I would share my thoughts and fears with my anchor that lived in the yellow quartz rock at the foot of the Lilac.

"Not so sure I can manage the raising of this boy," I would say.

And the comforting voice would reply, "Remember there is only one path. You've lived alone much too long. Raising Lucien will lift your head out of the sand. You will find new purpose in life. Ellen, the boy needs you."

"Needs me? What Lucien needs is a stable home with a father who is present and a mother who isn't too tired to listen."

"The boy needs you, Ellen," the voice repeated.

"The boy's got me," I said. "I'm doing my best and I just hope it is good enough."

My grandson didn't always throw a fit when it was time to go to school. Instead the poor lad would do his best to reason with me. There were many mornings when I would walk the two blocks down the road to the school with him. A sweet little boy with his blue eyes and curly brown hair, he would hold tight to my hand and say, "Gram, I wish you would listen to me. I wish you would try to understand. Gram, I really don't want to go to school."

"You have to go to school, Lucien," I would tell him.

[42]

"The kids laugh at me, Gram. I don't want to go to school," he would insist.

"You have to go to school, Lucien. Why are the kids laughing at you?"

"I don't know, Gram. But they do and I don't like it."

The first time Lucien told me about the other kids taunting him I was fit to be tied. When Carol came home from work that night I told her what he had said.

"Why are they laughing at him, Mom?" she asked me.

"I don't know, Carol. Apart from his tantrums when he doesn't want to go to school he's a good boy; cheerful and well-behaved. You know how much I love Lucien and it breaks my heart to say it but I think he's a little slow in the head. Kids can be cruel! You know that, Carol!"

"I'll talk to his teacher," she said. And that was the end of that.

By the time Lucien was eight years old the tantrums were fewer and far between. The morning arrived when he didn't want me to walk to school with him anymore. "It's just down the street, Gram. I can go by myself. The kids tease me. They call me a little baby 'cause I'm walking to school with my grandma."

I didn't want to but I knew I had to loosen my grip. I had no choice. I had to stop walking with him to school.

My new habit was to send him off to school on his own. Then I'd grab my bundle buggy and pull it along behind me as I walked. I'd keep my distance behind him so he couldn't' see me but my eye was always on Lucien until he turned into the school yard. Then I'd carry on up the street, turn at the corner and go into the Dominion Store to do some shopping. I did that every morning for several months. Those days I always had more food in the house than I knew what to do with.

Throughout the spring and summer I would make a point of doing my front yard gardening at the time when school was letting out for the day. Before watering the flowers I would do my weeding. Then I would take my trowel and loosen the earth around the rose bush and the peony plants. By the time I was standing there, hose in hand, watering the garden, school would be out and the children would be coming down the street on their way home.

Throughout the winter months I would time it just right in order to be in the driveway clearing away the snow when the school bell sounded.

I didn't have the cataracts then as I do now and my vision was just about okay. I could spot Lucien coming along down the sidewalk by the time he was a little more than a block away. I couldn't help noticing that while other children walked together in groups of two or three, Lucien would always be walking home from school by himself. While other children would be shouting and laughing, Lucien would walk head down in silence.

The temptation to turn off the water, put the hose aside and get out there to walk with my grandson was always with me. But I resisted the urge and stayed where I was. The other kids already thought he was a sissy and I didn't want to make things any worse for him than they already were. He never knew I was watching him in this way. No one knew. This was something I shared only with my rock beneath the Hummingtree.

In this way I was able to offer some protection to Lucien on his way to and from school. Of course I had no control over what took place in the schoolyard before classes started or during recess. I know he was teased. Lucien was a simple, trusting child and he would share with me in his own matter-of-fact way.

"They called me an idiot today, Gram."

"Who called you an idiot, Lucien?" I asked.

"The other kids. They called me an idiot 'cause they said I got nobody home upstairs. How come they say these things to me, Gram? We don't even have an upstairs in this house."

"Don't you pay one bit of attention to what those kids say to you, Lucien!"

I wanted to beat the tar out of those little brats. I wanted to teach them a lesson or two but my hands were tied. I hated to worry her but I did tell Carol about it. I felt like I had no choice because my daughter was his mother after all.

"I'll talk to his teacher," was all she would ever say to me about it.

The years went by in much the same way. I wanted to teach Lucien to stand up for himself, to protect himself from the endless jeers that came his way. I wasn't sure how to go about doing this.

While Lucien was away at school I spent many hours resting beneath my Hummingtree. I would lay my fears, my concerns and my frustrations on my rock while I recited my litany of needy questions. The answer was always the same. "He needs you, Ellen. Just be there for him and let him know he is loved."

"Maybe I should take him to a gym and get him some boxing lessons. Or maybe Karate would be a better idea. Or maybe I should go and talk to the parents of these rotten kids who won't stop picking on Lucien."

"No, Ellen," the rock beneath my Hummingtree insisted. "Just be there for him. Nothing else is required of you."

My Hummingtree had never let me down. I needed to keep the faith and know that the advice I received was what I needed to follow. But, I'm a willful woman. I decided that if I couldn't teach Lucien to fight back with his fists, I would teach him to fight back with words.

"Sing this song with me, Lucien," I would say. "Sing loud now! *Sticks and stones may break my bones but words will never hurt me!*"

I taught Lucien how to sing this song. We would sing it together. "Lucien," I said to him in the morning before he set off for school, "remember the song. If any of those kids give you a hard time just sing it loud and clear, okay?"

"Okay, Gram," he said.

I never did hear him singing though. "Hey retard!" they shouted. I would hear the teasing taunts of the cruel children and Lucien's silence would break my heart.

As he grew older the teasing continued but the bullies no longer gained satisfaction from words alone. They began picking at Lucien. They would form a circle around him and they would push him from one kid to another. I never saw this happen myself but Lucien told me about it.

"Did you push them back, Lucien?"

"No, Gram."

"You should push them back."

"Okay, Gram."

[47]

But, of course, he never did. I told Carol about it.

"I'll talk to his teacher," she said.

Lucien had more than his fair share of troubles in his short life but the day that stands out in my mind is that Tuesday six years ago when Lucien was only ten.

"He's a bit slow in the head," I said to my daughter again that morning.

"Learning difficulties, Mom! He has learning difficulties!"

That afternoon I was out in my front yard watering the plants just as I did every day. School had been let out and children were shouting, laughing and playing on the sidewalk as they passed my house on their way home. This day I did not see Lucien coming.

Soon the sidewalks were silent.   All the children had passed by and still there was no sign of Lucien. Panic started in my stomach and by the time it worked its way into my heart my legs had already gone into action. I ran the two blocks up the road to the school.

Lucien was not in the school yard.   He was not inside the school. Lucien was nowhere to be found. The teacher tried to calm me down. "He's probably just playing at a friend's house," she said.

I just stared at her. "Playing at a friend's house? Are you Lucien's teacher?"

"Yes, of course."

"Then you must know that Lucien has no friend."

"Come. We will talk to the principal," she replied.

The principal called the police. I went home and I called Carol. "I'm on my way home," she said.

I was fit to be tied. Lucien! Lucien! Where are you, my boy?

I had to do something but what could I do? I left the house and went out into the backyard. I sat on God's good earth beneath my Hummingtree. I prayed to my God in the yellow quartz rock. I prayed harder than I had ever prayed in my life. "Help me, God. Help me find my Lucien."

"Be still, Ellen," the voice whispered. "You will find him in the silence."

Not knowing what else I could do, I did as I was told. I sat beneath my Lilac and listened as the humming in the tree became louder and louder. I was lost in the humming when I began to see Lucien in my mind's eye. The woods! Lucien was in the woods!

I raced to the back gate, left my yard and followed the trail into the woods behind my house. "Lucien! Lucien!" I shouted as I ran.

At long last I heard my boy. "Gram! Help! Over here, Gram!"

I followed the voice through the deep woods until at last I could see him. *Thank you, God, for leading me to my boy.* Aloud I shouted, "I'm coming, Lucien. Gram is here!"

They had tied him to a tree. They had stripped him of his clothes and with clothesline rope they had tied my little Lucien to a tree. In black marker ink they had scrawled the words *PISSY SISSY* across his heaving chest.

"Help me, Gram!" he cried.

As I untied the rope I kept repeating, "It's okay, Lucien. It's okay. Gram is here. I will help you." I removed my old sweater and wrapped it around his shivering body. "Let's go home, son."

"I don't want to go to school anymore, Gram"

"I know, Lucien. I know."

I made my report to the police. I told Carol everything that had happened.

"I'll talk to his teacher," she said.

"No!" I shouted. "No more! This time I will talk to his teacher. We will find another school for Lucien; one where he fits in. I will not stand by for one more day and watch this boy be victimized by bullies."

Six years ago that is exactly what I did. Today Lucien thrives in his classroom where all the children are a bit slow in the head.

[51]

"They have special needs, Mom. Don't say slow in the head."

"All right, special needs! Anyway we are the ones who were slow in the head but thanks to my Hummingtree we are wiser today."

THREE

THREE:

Dream Beneath The Hummingtree:

At first it moaned and groaned but soon the thunder thrashed. It cracked the stillness of the back yard. It was a welcome interruption and my ears wanted to dance to its music. Was it finally going to rain? I sure did hope so. How strange it was to see flash lightning in the sky when the sun was still shining. I could not feel its welcome wetness yet but I could see a few drops of rain as they splattered from the leaves of the rose bush onto God's good earth.

My hands, especially my fingers, were hurting and that was usually a sure sign of rain. The old arthritis was playing up again. Some people have had the nerve to say it's all in my mind. I know. I've overheard the snide whispers behind my back. Anyway they are dead wrong. Rheumatoid arthritis is definitely a chronic, somatic condition. Sometimes I think the persistent pain in my hands is going to drive me clear out of my mind; if it hasn't already.

I set my trowel aside and with my tired hands on the ground I pushed myself up to a not quite erect standing position. Yes, my back ached but pure pleasure overwhelmed my pain. There was no denying that I loved working in the garden. It wasn't by accident that most of the plantings were perennial. Every year or two I would get busy with the mulching but in spite of my hard work the weeds were strong. They never lost their determination to flourish.

As usual that day I had been kneeling far too long on the ground. My arthritic knees were killing me. Yes, I used the foam rubber pad I had picked up at Dollarama as a cushion to place on the ground beneath my knees but sometimes my intended twenty minutes to work in the garden easily turned itself into two hours.

"People just don't realize how much industrious labour goes into keeping this garden so beautiful," I say to no one there.

My lovely roses and elegant lilies were in desperate need of a long, steady rain. I felt sad to see the backyard grass turning brown and ugly even though I had always kept plugging away throughout the dry summer in order to keep it watered and at least with some semblance of life. Maybe I just needed a good cry; hadn't had one in quite a long time. Just like nature and the small world around me I believed I was plain dry; dry of energy; dry of purpose. I was aware that I was living a self-serving life. There was no doubt in my mind that this did not serve me well at all.

When I leaned my head back to look up at the swirling sky I heard my tired, old neck creak and crackle. I was dismayed to see the dark clouds as they, like gigantic blackbirds, flew past overhead. At the rate the clouds were flying I was convinced they weren't going to stay around long enough to amount to a decent rainfall. No doubt it would just be another pitiful, little rainspit.

If it was up to me it would have rained three weeks ago. But there's no sense in me worrying about something I can't change. The good Lord knows how much we need the rain. It's not something within my power. Anyway as much as the rain is needed the weeding is important too.

Now the clouds have passed me by and the sun is smiling once more. I smile back and decide that since I'm finally up off the ground I will take a little rest; just a short break. I hate to admit, even to myself, that I'm not as young as I used to be.

The sun was a hot one that afternoon. I could feel my face starting to burn in spite of the fact that I was wearing my big, floppy gardening hat; its wide brim trimmed with yellow and blue plastic daisies. Yep, a ten minute break was all I needed. Then I'd be as good as new and ready to get back to work.

I made my way over to my white painted garden bench under the Hummingtree. This was my favourite place in the yard. Never mind just in the yard! This was my favourite place in the entire world. It was cooler there under the Lilac and this was my sanctuary; the place where I could commune with God through my yellow quartz rock.

I sat on my bench. I reached out my hand and caressed the rock. May as well keep the neighbours entertained by giving them something to talk about.

I knew what people in town thought of me.

"Oh, she's the crazy lady that talks to a rock," one would say.

"Rocks in the head!" says another.

It was no secret to me that others thought I was crazy carrying on conversations with a rock but by this point in my life I was way past caring what other people thought of me or what they said about me. My beautiful yellow quartz rock had been my best friend ever since I first discovered it under my Hummingtree more years ago than I care to remember. I'm sure I have already told you that I made the discovery the very day my father died. I was just a little girl and my Hummingtree was a plum tree then.

I've made lots of moves since then and so has my rock. For the last ten years my Hummingtree has been a lilac. When I was younger I used to sit on God's good earth and talk to my rock. Those are by-gone days. Now I need the support of my garden bench.

Yes, we've all heard the old saying that living alone is not all that it's cracked up to be. I've discovered that this old saying is a new reality. The fact is that I can go for days on end with nobody to share a cup of tea and a conversation. Oh, my daughter, Carol, calls when she can make the time but that's not often. Eleven years ago, when I was just fifty-seven, I used to see Carol often. Of course, she needed me then.

Every mother knows that kids always call when they need something. I would console myself by saying *no news is good news.*

No one needs me now. Carol used to drop my grandson, Lucien, off here at my house on mornings Monday through Friday. I'd take care of him all day each week day while she was away working at her much needed job in order to support her son. But I digress. I'm sure I've already told you a little about that time in my life. Lucien was a precious, wee boy but a handful at times, being just a little slow in the head. "He has special needs, Mom," Carol would insist.

She got so mad at me when I said he was slow in the head. "Learning difficulties! Don't say slow in the head! He has learning difficulties, Mom."

Special needs, learning difficulties, slow in the head; what's the difference? I mean it all means the same thing and why Carol got mad at me was beyond my comprehension. She knew very well how much I loved my only grandson. He was my boy.

Of course once he was old enough to go to school, his looking after didn't take up so very much of my time. Lucien is a teenager now and he has been going to this special school for a few years. He is much happier and better adjusted since starting attendance at the special school where he is forming friendships. I used to see him almost every day and now I practically never see him.

No, I don't see him often. I miss him.

My other daughter, Sandi, is all involved with her work. I understand. And it doesn't make a bit of difference whether I understand or not. The reality is that the kids are busy. I can't expect them to be running over here all the time.

I remember some words that I read in a book some time ago. They go like this. *Strong friendship doesn't need daily conversation; doesn't always need togetherness, as long as the relationship lives in the heart, true friends will never part.* Guess that's kind of how it is between me and my children. They are both good girls. They phone when they can find the time.

But living alone was never all that it's cracked up to be. It is nice though, sitting here on my bench. I'm blessed and grateful that I can commune through my rock any time of the day or night and just as often as I feel the need to do so. He is always there for me.

"Hello, God," I say.

My next door neighbour, Emma, has caught me more than once talking to God in my rock. When she questioned me the first time about what I was up to, I denied nothing. I told her I believed that God lives in the rock. Since that day she has avoided me. I miss her companionship very much but there is nothing I can do to change her views. I pretend I don't care.

Back to what I was telling you earlier, I was enjoying my rest on the garden bench but decided it was time to get back to work. Just as I was about to stand up, I could hear the humming in my rock. I could hear it clearly as it made its way up the trunk of the lilac. As always, the humming was a soothing sound. It relaxed me.

I decided I would not go back to work in the garden right away. Instead I would rest a little longer. I had no intention of going to sleep but I decided there would be no harm in just resting my eyes for a minute or two.

"It's too bad the rain is holding off for yet another day," I say to my rock. "You know this garden needs help. I could use some help myself, Lord. With these old, arthritic hands it's not always the easiest thing to haul that old garden hose around this big yard."

Now the humming was growing louder. I knew the sound was an invitation to become lost once again. I call it *getting lost* but the fact of the matter is when I lost myself in my Hummingtree's melody I found I was transported to exactly where I needed to be. It's almost as though if I want to be found, first I need to get lost.

Then I think of my grandson, Lucien, and the day he was lost. Then I think of the old hymn, *Amazing Grace. I once was lost but now I'm found; was blind but now I see.* The lyrics of this old song are right on the money when it comes to describing how I came to know where my Lucien was that day. Yes, indeed, it was just like that on the long ago day when my Hummingtree led me to Lucien who had been abandoned in the woods by those nasty, bullying boys.

Today was no exception. I allowed myself to become one with the humming. I could feel myself travelling as the soothing sound persisted. I felt the warmth of the sun and I knew it was shining upon my face but I had closed my eyes and couldn't see a thing. I had not closed my ears though and they could hear. My only roof was my Lilac Hummingtree but what I was hearing was the tap-tap of the rain on the roof.

Of course I knew rain couldn't tap on a tree and besides I knew that once I opened my eyes I could confirm that it wasn't even raining but I didn't doubt what I heard. No, not for one second did I question what my ears were receiving. I had absolute trust in the sounds that were emanating from my yellow quartz rock beneath my Hummingtree that day.

No, I was not asleep. I was not dreaming but I was being picked up and carried by an old memory and this remembrance was taking me somewhere. It was taking me to a place I didn't plan to visit that day. Indeed it was a place I did not want to visit that day but it's like that with my Hummingtree. It's like that with my God. He doesn't always give me what I want but I have learned from personal experience and sometimes through retrospect that he always gives me exactly what I need. He leads and I follow.

Some people have called me loony but I'm past caring about that. And now, just because I'm growing older, people think I'm getting senile. Or what's that fancy word they have for it these days? Alzheimer's! Yes, that's it! Some people think I have that strange disease with the even stranger sounding name. But what do they know?

What they don't know is that my Hummingtree has been taking me to places since I was a little girl. Nothing to do with my age!

Over the years I have learned to have faith and to trust that no matter where I am sent by my God through the yellow, quartz rock, whether it is a place I want to be or not, my presence there will be where I need to be. Indeed, whatever happens in that place will be in the best interest of all concerned.

"Where are you taking me today, Lord?" I asked my God in the yellow quartz rock.

"Listen to the rain, Ellen. Do you hear the rain on the roof?" My rock whispered.

"I do. I hear the rain."

I looked around me and I was no longer in my backyard. Through God's grace I was transported and I could see that I was in the old house. No, no, it's not the house I grew up in. It's the house I lived in with

Jerry many long years ago. It's the house where I resided when my daughters were little girls. It's where they played on the swing in the backyard and dressed their Barbie dolls in the basement rec room. It's where I sat on the ground beside my rock beneath the awesome Oak.

My rock asked, *"What do you see?"*

"I see my little girls," I said. "It's such a long time ago, Lord."

"Talk to me, Ellen. What else do you see?"

"The girls are asleep in their beds upstairs. It's pouring rain. I can hear the loud tap-tapping on the roof. I'm grateful that the kids sleep through the thunderous claps. Their eyes are closed to the swords of lightning that pierce their way through the ominous, dark clouds."

"How are you feeling, Ellen?"

"I'm afraid, dear Lord. But I don't dare let anyone know how scared I am. I don't want my kids growing up being fearful of thunder storms." I take a few moments and I walk through that old house. "Lord, I can see Jerry now."

"Tell me about it, Ellen."

"It's not a place I want to visit. Please God, let's leave this place. I'd rather forget."

"Tell me about it, Ellen."

[63]

As always I succumb to His will. "Okay, Lord, if you insist. I see myself climbing the stairs. I'm going upstairs to check on the girls. Through the open doorway I peer into their room and I see they are okay. They are sound asleep. I am grateful that the storm is not disturbing them at all. I go into the bathroom and that's when it happened.

"Tell me about it, Ellen."

"It's not a pretty story, Lord."

"Tell me."

"Well, it was a heavy rain that night. Thunder hammered my ears and lightning snaked its way throughout the house, white light flashing and frightening. After checking that the girls were okay in their shared bedroom I went into the bathroom. When I saw what was happening in that little room I freaked out and called for Jerry."

"Oh, my God! Jerry, come upstairs! Hurry Jerry!" I shouted.

I remember his frustration, his angry tone of voice. "Oh, for heaven's sakes, what do you want this time?" he shouted back.

More than anything else I didn't want to wake the girls from their sound sleep. I didn't want to shout but I was left without choice. My feet were glued to the floor and I couldn't make myself move. "Jerry, come upstairs!" I shouted again as the old house shook beneath the bellowing thunder.

"What now?" he moaned as he came up the stairs.

The constant drip, drip, dripping of the rainwater through the ceiling had formed a small lake on the bathroom's tiled floor. "The roof is leaking!" I shouted. "Do something!"

"What do you expect me to do?" he yelled back.

"Fix it!" I demanded.

"Do you know what time it is?" he hollered.

"It's time to fix this tired old roof!" I told him. "How many times have I asked you to check the attic in this old house? If you had checked it like I told you to, you might have seen signs of water damage and we wouldn't have Niagara in the bathroom tonight!"

"How am I supposed to get up into the attic?" he snarled.

Before I had a chance to answer he went into our bedroom, picked up the old, yellow, wooden chair and carried it into the bathroom. He was about to step up onto the chair when I shouted, "There's no way you can climb up into the attic with a stupid chair! Do you ever think? Get the step ladder for goodness sakes."

"If you know so much why don't you get it yourself?" he snarled.

[65]

He trounced downstairs and out to the garage to get the ladder. I went down to the basement where I found an old bucket and some dry rags.

Back upstairs I wiped up the flood the best I could, wrung the rags into the bucket and poured the water down the toilet before I put the bucket under the leak. Finally Jerry was there with the step ladder. He climbed up high enough to open the access to the attic in the bathroom ceiling. "Can't see a thing up here," he shouted. "It's dark as the devil!"

"For heaven's sakes get a flashlight! Do I have to tell you every single thing to do?"

He climbed down the ladder's steps then clomped down the stairs to the kitchen where he found the flashlight that was always kept in a cupboard drawer. By then the bucket was filling up. I emptied it down the toilet and set it under the leak again.

At last Jerry was there, this time with the flashlight. He climbed the ladder again. "Can't see a thing!" he shouted.

"Keep looking," I shouted back.

Then, "Okay, I can see it now. Water's coming in through the roof!"

"Geez, Jerry, tell me something I don't know!"

"It's leaking in by the vent in the roof."

"The roof is only ten years old!" I cried out.

"The roof is okay," he yelled. "It's the flashing around the vent. Probably just needs to have the sealant around it repaired. Supposed to do that every five years!" he told me.

I was amazed. "You know that? If you know that why hasn't it been done?"

"I forgot!" he said

"Idle idiot! That's just typical! And I guess I forgot to tell you to do it. Is there anything you can do on your own around here without having to be told?"

Jerry climbed down the ladder. "Yep, there's something I can do on my own all right! And maybe this is just the time to do it."

"Time to do what?" I asked.

"Time to leave!" he said. "I've had it with you! I've had it with all the crap. This leaking roof is the last straw! I'm outa here!"

"You're outa here? What on earth do you mean, Jerry? How can you be outa here? We are a family! We have kids to raise! Have you lost the good sense you were born with?"

Jerry packed a bag and left that very night. I know he went to her house.

He thought he kept the secret well but I knew. I'd known for a few months but I was afraid to broach the topic. Instead I had been living in denial for some time. Denial was a lonely place to live.

But now, abandoned and heartbroken, I lay alone, sobbing, on the bathroom floor. My tears mixed with the water that overflowed the bucket. I didn't care. I wanted to die.

"Let me drown, God. Let me just drown in this mess!"

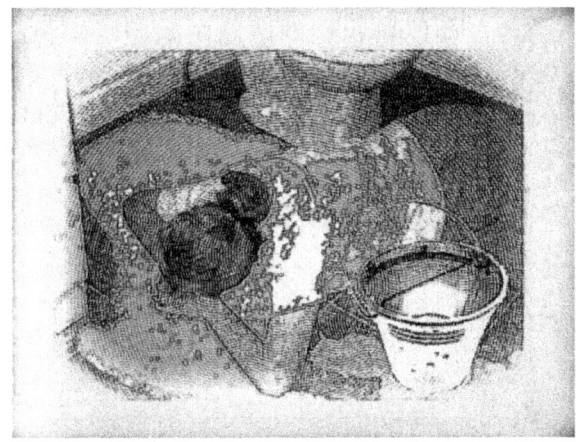

Just then I heard my little Sandi call out. "Mommy," she cried.

I picked myself up off the bathroom floor and went into the girls' shared bedroom. "I'm here, sweetheart. What's wrong, baby?"

"I'm scared, Mommy. The thunder woke me up."

"It's okay, Sandi. It's just a little storm. Nothing that won't pass."

"Will you sit with me until I get back to sleep, Mommy?"

"Yes, Sandi. I'm here. Go back to sleep now."

As I sat there with my little girl, I thought of years past. I remembered when Jerry and I were younger; before the marriage, before the kids, the bills, the house and the arguments. He loved me then and

[69]

God knows throughout the marriage he always loved his children. Everything was okay for the longest time but that was before he had the affair with that meddling marriage breaker.

I remembered a time when Jerry would say to me, "I love you, Ellen." His promise was deathless. He assured me of his undying love.

Ha! He'll be back!

I pulled myself together as best I could. *He'll be back. My Jerry is not going to abandon me and the kids. No, of course he won't. He'll be back!"*

I sat on the side of Sandi's bed. I closed my tired eyes and waited for my husband to return. Soon I could hear my little girl's soft, sleeping breath.

I open my eyes. The sun is shining. I look around and see my trowel lying on the ground beside the rose bushes where I've left it. I look up at the beautiful purple Lilac overhead. She still hums and I know God is with me. I speak to my rock, "He never came back!"

"I know, Ellen."

"Never did get that roof fixed! Had to put up with that for more than a year before I was finally able to take my girls and move into the rent-geared-to-income apartment."

"I know, Ellen."

[70]

"He never paid a penny of child support."

"I know."

"Living alone is not all that it's cracked up to be."

"You are never alone, Ellen. I am always with you."

"I know," I say. "Thank you, Lord."

With my God's reassurance that I am never alone I felt a little better but feelings of abandonment were often not far. Jerry left me and I struggled as a single mother after that day.

And long ago when my father left my mother he also left me to grow up without a daddy. I wanted a father like all the other children had. It is said that people can get used to anything and it is true that I got used to being left; to being abandoned, and with that I lost my ability to believe that anything in life was lasting.

The clouds have all disappeared. The summer sky is clear blue. No sign of rain. It's time to get back to work. I plop my floppy, old, wide-brimmed hat back onto my head, get up from my garden bench and head back to the rose bushes. I reach down to retrieve the trowel. With a heavy sigh I kneel on the soft earth.

FOUR

FOUR:

Ellen's Roots Beneath The Hummingtree:

I remember I was sitting on God's good earth beneath the Hummingtree when it happened. I was fifteen years old. Feeling bored and restless, I confided in my yellow quartz rock. The soft response was silent thunder. Even at that early tender age I knew better than to question His advice. The good Lord had never steered me wrong before. I didn't think He was about to start then.

"Go my child, go down into the cellar. When you get there you will know what to do. You will find what you need there. Go my child."

As instructed, I lifted myself from the soft, warm ground and stood up. Mom had gone out shopping with my aunt and there was no one home that day to question my actions. Alone in the quiet I descended the stairs into the basement of my mother's old house. I felt grateful no one was there to watch me.

Somehow, just as the good Lord had said, I knew what needed to be done. I walked across the basement's concrete floor to the back block wall. I stopped walking when I was not far from the dusty, old, coal furnace. This part of the wall was covered with a layer of plastic material. Yes, I knew what I needed to do. I set to work. Had anyone seen me clawing at the dirty basement wall covering they would have thought I

[73]

was insane. Mom would have had a fit at the mess I was making as I tore off the old, yellowed plastic that had covered the cellar's back wall.

Sure enough, as He had assured me it would be, there it was. His promise was sure and the book was there exactly where He had said it would be. Leaving the shredded plastic in its piles on the basement floor, I carried Daddy's old journal with me across the basement floor, up the cellar stairs and out to the backyard. The journal was wrapped tightly in a strange leather-like material that I thought might be the hide of an animal. I could feel its power pulsing through my trembling hands.

Though I was just a teenager I had earlier heard relatives talking about the deathless legend attached to my father's journal. I had no idea why it was hidden in the cellar or who did the hiding. Legend taught that the journal was first discovered under a boulder soon after his death. Since then no one had been able to hold it in their hands long enough to remove the strange wrapping in order to read it.

I was having no problem holding it in my hands on this day of discovery. My mother had told me that my father's journal was cursed and best hidden away. Was it my mother who had buried it inside the cellar's wall?

My mother had also told me my father's boots were haunted. She couldn't hold them without weeping but I thought her tears fell because she felt lonely since her husband had abandoned her. Was I mistaken? Was it the actual touch of the boots that caused the tears to flow?

Others said that his knife was haunted. My aunt told me that even though his knife was extremely sharp to the touch it couldn't cut butter.

I had heard all these stories but I didn't know where the truth was hidden. I was only five when Daddy took off. I never really knew my father.

Fate decreed it was time to become better acquainted with my dad. I sat on God's good earth beneath the Hummingtree. I removed the animal hide beneath which his journal had been hidden. With trembling hands I opened the book. Though faded with time I could see that my father's handwriting was legible. With anticipation I started to read.

Today it is many years later and as I write this story I am undecided as to whether I should tell you in my own words what my father had written or whether I should let my daddy's words tell their own story. I allow memory to take me back to that day when I, a young teenager dressed in blue jeans, floral sleeveless cotton blouse, white bobby socks and saddle shoes, sat down on God's good earth beneath my Hummingtree and asked for guidance.

"You have your own story to tell, Ellen. Let your father's words be what they are. Let the tale be told as he wanted it to be shared."

"Thank you, Lord," I had responded back then and this memory tells me today how I must write things down.

My decision is made. Just as God instructed many years ago I will let the journal entries be just what they are. In this way, if this story ever has a reader that person will hear it as my daddy wanted it to be told.

The first entry was written in the long-ago summer of 1919; twenty-three years before I was born.

August 1, 1919: My name is Leon MacPherson. I was born sometime in 1899 and that makes me somewhere near twenty years old today. I'm a trapper. I was born down south but today you could try to find me up near James Bay. You can try but you won't find me. No one will find me because I don't want to be found. I live in the bush and I eke out my living trading furs with the James Bay Cree. I try to stay clear of the trading posts but they do exist. There is Waskaganish that the English call Rupert House. There's Chisasibi that the English call Fort George.

There are others too but I choose to trade directly with the Cree. They are good people. Lucky for me, most of them are bilingual. Sure, they have their own language but quite a few can speak some English. The Cree people have something that I need. The Bible says, "Seek and ye shall find." Well, I've been seeking but I haven't found what I'm looking for yet. I'm bound and determined to find it though. I won't give up the search until I do.

I've been told that to find what I need I have to stay still and it will come to me. I can't see a lot of truth in that so I will keep up the chase.

When I allowed myself to visualize my father, just twenty years old; only five years older than I am when I first read his journal, I just wanted to cry. I realized how much like him I am. He was a seeker. What was I that long ago day, if not someone seeking answers, seeking truth and wanting to understand who I am meant to be and who I can one day become?

Captive of my father's words, I continued to read. I could see that the second entry was written by Daddy several months after his first.

December 24, 1919: *It's Christmas Eve. I'm very cold even though I'm far inland. The Nuuchcimiihc liyuu, meaning* Inland Person, *are hunters. They hunt the caribou and they do some trading with the inland fur-trading posts. They are generous people and have provided me with geese, fish and hare. I stay clear of the James Bay fur-trading posts but the Cree people sometimes, though seldom, visit the post where they trade for goods they can easily transport.*

It's Christmas but that doesn't mean much to me. I'm not a religious person. Sure, I know all about the birth of Jesus. And the Anglican missionaries were often successful in instilling the notion of a Christian God in the minds of the Cree. They did this by connecting it to the notion of a powerful spirit known as Manitou which interpreted means "master of all

[77]

spirits". As for me, I prefer the notion of Manitou and I prefer the Cree translation which is "master of animal spirits".

Up to this point in my life animals have done more for me than people have ever done. Taking everything into consideration I confess I am surprised that the Cree people will deal with me. Whatever else I am, I'm still a white man, and the only things the white man has given to the Cree are whooping cough epidemics, government agents and prospectors.

My feet are warmed. My feet are warmed because of the boots I wear. These boots my Cree friends made for me will probably last forever. Rituals were carried out on these very boots. They are blessed or they are cursed depending entirely upon the intentions of the one holding the boots.

I'm warmly wrapped but I'm damn near freezing. It's not a somatic thing. My mind wanders and my spirit searches for what it knows it needs. The soul knows. But it's not telling; at least not today.

So it's true that the boots could be cursed as I'd heard the story of the legend repeated but now I understand that this curse may be only because the holder of the boots has less than good intention. I wondered why no one had, until now, told me that the boots could also be blessed. Learning that my father was a man of faith warmed my heart just as his boots warmed my Daddy's wandering feet.

I could no sooner stop reading his journal entries than I could stop breathing. Again I could see that a few months had passed before he penned his next entry. By its date I could see that it was written long ago in the early spring of 1920.

April 15, 1920: I was visited this morning by a Cree Indian. He informed me he is a Warrior of the Rainbow. *He said to me, "Before it is too late, let me teach you reverence for the Earth. Band with us and become a* Warrior of the Rainbow."

This wise man taught me that there will come a time when the Earth will be ravaged of its resources. The ocean will be blackened and streams poisoned. The deer will drop dead in its tracks and the birds will no longer be able to fly.

My Cree friend told me about an old lady from the Cree tribe. "She is named Eyes of Fire." *he said. She prophesied that because of the Yo-ne-gis, meaning white man's greed, there will come a time when the fish will die in the streams, birds will fall from the sky and trees will no longer exist.*

"A day will come," my friend said, "when white man's knife will no longer cut." Then he asked me for my hunting knife. I did as I was bid. My Cree friend honed my knife on a yellow quartz rock until its edge was razor sharp.

He said to me, "This knife is like a white man's tongue; sharp as a two-edged sword. But white man

[79]

speaks with forked tongue and his knife does not cut justice. White man has turned away from the Great Spirit. The Warriors of the Rainbow will be the keepers of the legend and the culture; the ancient tribal culture, "

Is this why I was told that the knife couldn't cut butter? Things were beginning to fall into place and make a little more sense to me now. I continued reading and a growing sense of closeness to my father nourished my soul.

After the visit from this Warrior I knew I could stop searching for what I needed. Soon I would no longer be lacking. My needs would be met by the Great Spirit. But, first, there was something I needed to accomplish.

I am blown away by my father's words. So much that was prophesied by the Warriors of the Rainbow had already taken place. And as I paused in my reading I wondered what it was that my father felt he needed to accomplish. Mesmerized by his words I began reading again. Starved for understanding, I couldn't read fast enough. I wondered why more than five years passed before he made his next entry.

September 21st, 1925: Since my visit from the Warrior of the Rainbow, I am learning that the Ancient Being called Great Spirit is full of compassion, understanding and love. Now I am also a Warrior of the Rainbow. I am the only white man who has been honoured by this proud label and I am learning to make *my path straight; right with the world. I am learning to pray to the Great Spirit with a love that flows like a magnificent mountain stream.*

One day this stream will flow along the path to the ocean of life and I will be able to feel joy. I will be free of petty jealousies. Happiness will flow into my heart and I will become one with the entire human race. I will find strength in solitude where once I found nothing but loneliness.

Strength in solitude? I had never considered such a possibility. As I read my father's writings I was beginning to understand that my future was filled with new and wonderful possibilities. Maybe being alone, and even feeling alone when in the company of others, is not the terrible thing I had thought it was. My father was the teacher and I was his student. The concept of the *power of one* was something I had never considered before. I was intrigued as I resumed my reading.

For sixteen years I will live in solitude. I will commune with nature and be one with the Earth. When sixteen years have passed I will leave this place. I will travel south to the place where my life journey began. I will take a wife and I will have a child.

This child will be able to run free and enjoy the treasures of Mother Earth. She will respect the powers of the plants and animals. These things I believe and so it will be.

Oh, my goodness. Now I am aware that long before I made my presence known on this earth my father knew I would be born. Was my daddy a prophet? My heart is pounding, my thoughts racing as I allowed the realization of my father's prophecy to be accepted as my reality. When he wrote these words my father was a young man but now I realize that he was, indeed, an old soul with special prophetic gifts. At fifteen years of age, as I continued to read, I hoped I could live up to those things my father decreed about me; that I would always respect plants and animals; that I would enjoy the treasures of Mother Earth in freedom.

Nearly fifteen years pass before my father writes his next journal entry.

August 12, 1940: The time has come. I will leave this place. I will travel far from James Bay and return to the place where I was born. Great Spirit has told me that upon my return I will meet a kind woman who will find love in her heart to share with me. Great Spirit speaks to me through the great yellow quartz boulder that sits beneath the tall pine. This pine hums and calms my spirit.

I will miss my boulder but Great Spirit has assured me that this rock will be with me wherever I may travel. Great Spirit further promises me that upon my transition from this life to one that is greater I will leave behind a yellow quartz rock. This rock will appear beneath a Hummingtree. It will be seen and heard by my child alone. Just as Great Spirit speaks to me through the boulder, the Ancient of Ancients will speak to my child when I am no longer in the flesh. This is the promise upon which I hang my faith.

I'm blown away by my father's prophecy. Now that I have my very own yellow quartz rock and now that my plum tree has transformed into my very own Hummingtree I realize how very blessed I am to be my father's daughter. And I am thrilled when I begin reading the next entry which is written just one day after the date of my arrival on earth.

August 13, 1942: Today I live as a white man but my heart beats to the drum of the Cree traditions. I am truly blessed by the Great Spirit. The promise of the rock has been kept. I have married a kind woman. Her name is Eva Campbell but I have given her my name along with my heart. Her new name is Eva MacPherson and yesterday she gave me the gift of a child.

We have named her Ellen Angela MacPherson. I love my wife and I love my child but I do not rest easy on the concrete paths of the city. I yearn for the wilderness. I am a Warrior of the Rainbow but too often I feel swallowed up by the big smoke of the smoldering hot city streets.

Tears drip from my chin. To know that my father loved me is a gift. This knowledge fills a hole inside of me that I didn't even know existed. Yes, he did abandon my mother and me. But even though I am just a teenager when I read his words for the first time, I am gaining an inkling of understanding about his actions. I am becoming ready to accept that he was not the dead-beat dad; the bad person clothed in evil as others had professed and as I had come to believe.

I was just five years old the day my daddy once again left our city home.

September 3, 1947: *I have to leave. Though it breaks my heart to hear the sharp, angry tongue of a woman disappointed and abandoned by a man she thought she could trust I know I must leave. I cannot bear to feel the wetness of my little Ellen's tears against my hand as she holds tightly and cries, "Please daddy, don't go away."*

She is only five years old, a baby. I could not go but I had to leave. I was suffocating. I yearned for the bush. I needed to breathe the clean, fresh air. I needed to hear the wise voices of my Cree brothers.

I remember the day my daddy left me alone to hear my mother's cries. He left me and for ten years I felt emptiness that through this reading was just beginning to heal. I see that his next journal entry is quite a few years later.

By 1953 I would have been eleven years old.

March 16, 1953: *Another winter is over. It has been a long, difficult time. I fear my journey on this Earth will soon be finished. I am not well. My Cree friends invited me into the sweat lodge. The extreme heat has cleansed the toxins out of my body and killed the bacteria. More important than this physical* *revitalization is the spiritual renewal with which I am blessed and also the purification of my mind which allows me to see more clearly.*

The hot coals on forked sticks burned hot and bright. Sweet grass was burned and its incense filled my being with healing fragrance. The wise old Cree lady began to sing, "Man is coming in with his body. It is sacred." She sang this song four times.

In the sweat lodge my journey stretched before me. With clarity I could envision my footsteps and the direction they must take.

I left the sweat lodge and began my preparations.

I realize then that this must be when my daddy was once again coming back into my world. I remember the day very clearly. In spite of all the criticism I had overheard, the nasty words spoken against him by my aunt, my mother and others, I remember that the day of my father's return was, for me, a happy day. As I continued to read I was filled with delight knowing that, in spite of all outward appearances, my father did, indeed, care about me.

With this knowledge I read my father's last journal entry.

October 24, 1953: *I have said good-bye to my Cree brothers. I will return to my wife, Eva, and my child, Ellen. She will not be a little girl much longer. Ellen will be a woman soon; a wise woman mature* *enough to accept the inheritance I will leave for her alone.*

Time is of the essence. This will be my last entry in this journal. I will finish writing my words and then I will wrap my journal in the skin of a caribou. There it will remain in safe-keeping until the day it is discovered by my daughter.

The Great Spirit has assured me that once I place my journal beneath the yellow quartz boulder it will be discovered by Eva. Afraid of what she may find within the journal Eva will remove it from beneath the rock. She will hide it behind the yellow plastic that hangs from the back wall of the cellar beneath the house in which they live.

Upon my death it is decreed by Great Spirit that Ellen will first discover the yellow quartz rock. She will commune with the Ancient of Ancients through the rock as I have done in the wilderness of my mind and of my country. She will sit beneath a tree as I sit beneath my Pine on the soft Earth and she will hear the humming as it rises up the trunk of the tree until it fills the branches that protect her soul. Great Spirit will provide my daughter with her own Hummingtree.

In my life-long search I found what everyone else is always trying to find. I found the greatest gift of all. I found "the peace that passeth understanding". This inner peace will one day be discovered by my daughter. That day may not come until my child is a wise, old woman, but that day will surely be when Great Spirit decrees.

My journal and its legend will be all that remains of me when I leave this good Earth. My name is Leon MacPherson. I am fifty-four years of age. I will die in the arms of my beloved Eva. I have given her great heartache in this life and for this I offer deep regret. She is a good woman. While most women would not, The Great Spirit assures me she will welcome me home. My Ellen will grow up and she will say, "I never really knew my father."

And so it will be.

And so it was. My father was a prophet and he is gifting me with the awareness that peace of mind will be mine one day. I haven't yet learned to accept this gift but since my father believed one day I will have this experience; I make this my belief also.

I closed my father's journal. I could not stop the torrent of tears that fell from my eyes. Now I had greater understanding. Now I had greater appreciation for the gift of the yellow quartz rock beneath my Hummingtree. Holding the journal in my hands I felt blessed knowing it had been bequeathed to me upon my father's death; a time when I was only twelve years old with no awareness of the journal's existence.

I neither understood my discovery of the rock nor the powerful humming of the tree. I did not know until today that these things were my inheritance. This is my father's legacy. These things were the gifts from my father in order that I would be able to talk to God as he had done when he lived in the wilderness.

As I sat beneath my Hummingtree I wondered if God thought I was too young to understand all that my father had to share at the time that he died. Could that be the reason He did not lead me to the yellow plastic wall in the cellar upon the day of my daddy's death but instead waited until today?

I hold his journal close to my heart. I honour his memory and I am grateful for the inheritance he has given me. Though he was not a physical part of many of my growing-up childhood years I am warmed by the knowledge that he always and forever holds me, his only child, near to him. He has bequeathed to me wisdom, knowledge and love. He has taught me that God is not far from me; that He is always and forever as close as I will allow Him to be.

At fifteen I have no doubt Great Spirit spoke to my father through the yellow quartz boulder beneath the stately Pine tree. He was a Warrior of the Rainbow. I cannot be less.

Having read his journal I can no longer say I never really knew my father. Though he was miles away throughout most of my childhood, I now understand that he was always with me in spirit. He always will be. This day I found my roots beneath my Hummingtree and now that I am soon an old lady, I share my story with you.

FIVE

FIVE:

***Terrible Ticking*:**

I was in the kitchen preparing my breakfast this morning when it started. At first, to my old ears, it was almost inaudible but, like an unwanted intruder, the soft tick, tick, tick, pushed its way into my maddened mind. I leaned over the sink, opened the kitchen window and, without missing a beat, a sharper, clicking sound wafted in with the morning breeze. *What on earth is that terrible ticking? Just what I don't need; to be entangled in another mystery!*

I turned my back on the open window and carried my bowl of Cheerios out of the kitchen and into the sunny dining room where I sat on the seat of the ladder-backed chair at the old, round, pedestal table. As I ate my breakfast the tick, tick, tick, transformed into a tick, tackle, tick; tick, tackle, tick. As it became louder it also became slower until it resembled a mournful moan like a funeral lament.

At my age I have learned to ignore disruptions created by my neighbours. I'm not nearly as curious, or call it nosy if you must, as I used to be. Like my father before me, I have found strength in solitude. I cherish my time spent alone with my thoughts being my only companion.

As a rule I am able to tune out unwanted sounds, sights and other worldly things. By the time I have somehow managed to reach the age of sixty-eight I have learned to like living alone; to like my peace and quiet; but this intrusion could no longer be ignored. The rhythm picked up. Tick, tackle, tick had been replaced by tackle, tick, tick; tackle, tick, tick.

I'm suddenly reminded by this racket of New Year's Eve celebrations when I was a young child. Our family and all families in the neighbourhood, at the stroke of midnight, would come out onto their front lawns or verandahs shouting Happy New Year! They would all join together to make a loud noise by banging pots together or shaking tambourines or beating on a pie plate with a spoon. Tick, tackle, tick. *Is someone banging a tin drum?*

I carried my empty cereal bowl back out into the kitchen where I placed it into the stainless steel sink atop the pile of dirty plates, bowls, cutlery, pots and pans from last night's supper. I couldn't do up the dishes last night. The house had been too hot. The high humidity wore me down and I just could not find the energy to wash up. Not for the first time in my life, I wished I had an underling, a magical maid, a kind soul who would come in once in a while to help with these bothersome household chores.

My daughter, Carol, would surely be surprised to see these dirty dishes piling up in my sink. Both Carol and Sandi know I am usually very fussy. I am the one who taught them the old adage that there is a place for everything and, to set a good example, I always did my best to keep everything in its place.

[92]

Neatness and cleanliness were important to me and my usual habit was to keep the house as neat as a pin. In fact, when they were little girls sharing the joys and sorrows of growing up together, I often made my daughters' little lives a misery with my nit-picking fussiness.

But this hot weather had its way with me last evening and so the dishes sat soaking in the sink in water that by now had turned as cold as the cruel clock-like ticking. By now the ticking is no longer a sorrowful, grieving rhythmic wail. Now it is a demanding, terrible ticking. Tack, tack, tack! Tack, tack, tack!

Enough! I'll see who is making this racket! I'll soon put an end to this!

I walked out into my backyard's morning sunshine. From my place on the deck I could see my next door neighbour, trowel in hand, working in her vegetable garden. She didn't seem to be disturbed at all by the terrible ticking.

I didn't usually initiate conversation with my long-time neighbour who, I knew, did her best to ignore me, but this ticking irritation gave me the encouragement I needed. "Emma," I shouted. "Where is all the noise coming from?"

"What noise?" my neighbour asked.

"You don't hear the loud ticking sounds?" I asked her.

In silent response, Emma simply shook her head in despair.

Bad enough she hears me talking to God who lives in my yellow quartz rock; now she thinks I am hearing imaginary ticking bombshells. Surely I am not imagining this ruckus!

I looked all around and could see no out-of-the-ordinary signs. Still I hear the ticking but its notes are lengthening. At once I am reminded of the folkloric banshee. Is there a message for me in this incessant, ticking howl of sorrow? Surely it is not an imaginary wail of self-pity?

Am I the only one who hears these strange sounds? Has the banshee come to warn me of impending death? Whose death? My own? No, surely not yet! Surely not!

Am I losing the good sense I was born with? Have I already lost it?

I decide there is only one reasonable course of action to take. I will sit on my bench beside my yellow quartz rock. I will be safe beneath my Hummingtree. I will ask God, my reliable rock, what is required of me.

With trepidation I tread lightly on the cement steps which wend their way through my glorious, summer garden to the bottom level of the terraced backyard. As I approach my bench I see it. Yes, I do see it but what on earth is it?

What is that big, dark spot on the grass? It looks like a hole. Nonsense! Who would come into my back yard and dig such a hole? What vandals would waste their time on such a useless task? Yes, maybe my neighbor is accurate in her diagnosis of me. Maybe I have lost it altogether. If not, what trick of the mind is this?

As I drew closer to my place of refuge I could see that it was, indeed, a hole in the ground. My lawn has been dug up and torn apart. *What scoundrel is responsible for this vandalism?*

I was standing now at the edge of the hole which was at least a foot wide. This was far too huge a hole to have been created by any garden critter such as a mole. No, indeed, this looked like the work of a human. Only a deranged person would vandalize my beautiful lawn in this manner.

But who? Who did this dirty deed? I turned my head and looked in all directions. Other than my neighbor, Emma who worked in her own garden, there was no one else in sight.

But the sound; the horrible, by now deafening, ticking sound could not possibly have human origin. I felt scared to death. Fear forbade it but I willed myself to overcome the dread and peer down into the blackness. It was a very deep hole. The loud and distinct ticking sound was coming up from its depths. By now it was a heart-wrenching sound. Tiiiiiick, tiiiiiiick, tiiiiiiiiick, tiiiiiiiiiick; each tick lasting a little longer than the one before.

How can my neighbour not hear the dire, dreadful decibel that is threatening to fill my body and my anxious brain?

At once I want to sit on my bench. I want to be sheltered under the umbrella of my Hummingtree. I need to feel and hear the reassurance of my heavenly Father. But how do I get around this deep hole to reach the safety of my bench? I want to sit in peace but how can I do this? I do not want my bedroom-slippered feet to be dangling over this horrific, hellish hole.

Then I notice there is a spot in front of the bench where I can stay grounded. Thanks be to God, this very spot is adjacent to my rock. With cautious, careful steps I make my way around the hole to this perceived place of sacred safety.

I sat myself down on my bench. With my feet firm on the ground I leaned my anxious body away from the depth of the hole and over the rock which rests beneath the purple Lilac. Filled with fear my voice is shaking but *"Hello God,"* I say.

I waited to hear the tree's humming. Strange; my lilac is silent. *Has God forsaken me?* All I can hear is the roar of the tiiiiiiiiick, tiiiiiiiiiick, tiiiiiiiiiiick rising from the depths of the hole.

I stretched my old body and leaned lower until I was low enough to touch my ear to the yellow quartz rock. *"Are you there, God? It's me, Ellen, and I'm very frightened."*

At last I could hear a faint hum. It was barely audible above the harsh, constant clack of the terrible ticking. *"Is it the banshee come for me, Lord? Are my mother's Gaelic ancestors calling for me?"*

The humming seemed bound to the base of the Lilac. I could feel its struggle as it attempted to make its way up the Hummingtree's trunk. I could feel the tingle of the hum in my feet. In my leaning over to talk to my rock I'd allowed my legs to move toward the hole until my slippered-feet were in a perilous position. My feet dangled over the hole. Then, with terror, I watched one of my slippers leave my foot bare and fall down, down, down into the depths of the black hole.

[97]

"Has my time come, Lord? Is my old soul in jeopardy?"

The humming was doing its utmost to be heard over the traumatic tiiiiiiiiiiiiick, tiiiiiiiiiiiiiick, tiiiiiiiiiiiiiiiick.

"Help me, God," I prayed. At long last, the humming sound was winning the battle. It made its way up the trunk of the purple Lilac and spread itself out into its branches and blossoms.

The humming drummed out the wailing beat of the terrible tick. As the humming increased, the depth of the hole was lessened. Soon I could see my slipper as it lay on its side on the floor of the chasm. The floor was rising like a cage in an old elevator shaft.

"Was it the female spirit after my soul? Was it the banshee coming to take me home to you, dear God?"

"Yes, Ellen," God responded, *"it was the terrible ticking banshee but you need worry no longer. She has put up a good fight but all is in order now."*

I could barely hear the ticking now. No bomb was going to explode this day. I sat there feeling quite dazed as I listened to the quiet, rhythmic tick, tick, tick but even this small tick was soon hidden beneath the soothing, humming warmth that reached down from the branches of the Lilac and wrapped me in its charismatic calm.

I watched the floor of the hole as it climbed higher and higher. At last the hole was gone and my slipper lay strewn on the green grass in front of my garden bench. The ticking ceased. And even the loud humming departed leaving me alone in the garden with my yellow quartz rock. I leaned over and asked, *"Why was she coming, Lord? Had I done something to displease you?"*

"The battle between good and evil is a constant one, Ellen. I know you were afraid. More than this I know that in your fear you came to me. Your unfaltering faith was strong enough to send the ticking banshee on her way. It's not your time yet, Ellen. You still have much to achieve on this saddened earth."

"I'll do my best, Lord. Thanks for coming to my rescue."

I leaned over and patted my yellow quartz rock. I looked up at the beautiful blossoms over my head. *"It's a lovely tree,"* I thought. *"I thank you, God, for my Hummingtree."*

I picked up my errant slipper, placed it back onto my foot and stood up. It was quiet now. The only sounds to be heard were the chirping robins and the occasional mournful cry of the loon as it flew overhead.

I left my bench beneath the Hummingtree and made my way back to the cement steps. I began my climb toward the house. As I crossed the yard to my kitchen door I noticed Emma, my neighbour, staring over the fence at me. I mutter to myself as I prepare to enter the house to wash the dishes piled up in the kitchen sink. *She thinks I'm nuts. I'm sure of it!* And then for just a second I had to ask of myself, *is she right? Am I nuts? Am I losing it? Is old age robbing me of the good sense I was born with?*

Then I heard my neighbour call. "Are you okay, Ellen?"

"Good morning, Emma," I respond. "Of course I'm okay. Why do you ask?"

"I heard you talking to the rock again. I couldn't help but overhear. Ellen, I would be happy to help you. I could give you the name of a good doctor. I'll even drive you to your appointment if you will just make one. I do care about you, Ellen. We've been neighbours for many years now and it worries me when I see you talking to that rock."

"Nothing for you to worry about, Emma," I assured her. "I've told you before and I will tell you again I'm not just talking to a rock. I'm talking to God."

"I know you think God lives in that rock, Ellen, but can't you just try to be reasonable?"

"Reasonable, Schmeasonable! Ye of little faith! God is omnipresent. Do you know what that means, Emma? It means He is present everywhere simultaneously; all at once. Don't you get it? Don't you know that if God wants to live in my rock He can live in my rock?"

I watched my neighbour as she bowed her head and shook it in despondency.

"Don't be sad for me, Emma." I told her. "The ticking, wailing banshee came for me this morning but God rescued me as I sat on my bench beneath my Hummingtree. It's God's truth I'm telling you, Emma."

"Okay, Ellen, have it your way," my neighbour sighed before going back to her gardening.

I went into the house. As I stood at the kitchen sink I turned on the hot water tap, put a couple of drops of Sunlight into the water. I watched as it covered the dirty dishes of last night and this morning. I washed them and rinsed them until they sparkled before I stacked them on the kitchen counter rack. Sometimes I like to air dry the dishes but this morning I decided they had filled my kitchen counter for long enough. I would dry them with a towel. Just as I reached for the blue, cotton tea towel hanging over the stove's oven door handle my ears were assaulted by a loud and distinct ticking sound.

Oh, no, not again! Back off banshee! You are not welcome here today!

I stood there feeling almost paralyzed on my own kitchen floor. Tea towel in hand, my eyes darted around the room. The origin of the ticking was definitely inside the kitchen; not coming from the backyard as it had been earlier.

And then I could only stand there and laugh aloud at my own foolishness when, at last, I realized my blunder. As I'd reached over to the stove to retrieve the dish towel my bumbling arthritic hand had bumped against the stove's timer. It was set to tick for a good ten minutes.

Silly old fool! Living alone is not all it's cracked up to be! It's only nine on a summer's morn and already you've had more than enough adventure for one day!

SIX

SIX:

Bear With Me:

Though I've swallowed twenty years it still feels like it happened yesterday. I still get a lump in my throat when I remember those long ago October days. My heart soared with the raven when my grandson, Lucien, was born that morning. Two days later my mother died.

Too much for one week! Too much!

That sad afternoon of my mother's passing I tried to savour the morning's moments when I travelled with the raven far above the woes of the world. It's not as though I wanted to be reminded of the beliefs held by my Irish ancestors. Had I not already suffered enough remorse because of the terrible ticking, wailing banshee? But, for me, there was no escaping the knowledge that my dear mother had shared with me. She told me that my father had confided that the raven was revered by my ancient family as a spiritual figure of God. Though my mother scoffed at this notion, I did not question what, to me, felt like truth.

Unlike my father, Leon MacPherson, my mother had always been frightened by what she called the old myths. "Old housewives' tales!" she would exclaim when my father attempted to share his truth. She knew his journal was bequeathed to me but, unbeknownst to me, she kept it covert. I didn't find that

[104]

well-hidden journal until several years had passed after my father's death.

Why did she keep my father's journal hidden? Why did my mother do that?

I didn't know the answer to the question then. Now that she is gone I will never know for sure but I think my mother's fear of the myths was why she hid her husband's journal on the day of his death.

Once discovered, his journal meant the world to me. My father's greatest gift to me before he commenced his journey into the afterlife was a deeper understanding of my yellow quartz rock's presence beneath the Hummingtree.

My father had died and now my mother was dead. Even though I was a woman in my forties I felt like an orphaned child. Unlike my father, she had left no journal, no memoirs, nothing to help me to understand her choices, her decisions, and her life.

What will constitute my inheritance from my mother? Her old Bible perhaps?

My mother always wanted me to read passages from the Bible. Bless her heart, she was a good mother, but she was always worried that I would tread my father's spiritual path into a foreign world where she could not find a comfortable pew.

In my early teen years I talked to God through my rock. Whenever I felt the need for affirmation, for counsel or for comfort I would sit upon God's good earth and commune with Him through my yellow quartz rock. He was always there for me as I, the seeker, visited beneath the Hummingtree.

"What are you doing, child?" she would question. "You can't be sitting under the plum tree talking to a rock!"

"God talks to me through the yellow quartz rock, Mom," I would tell her. I wanted to reassure her that I was not a little slow in the head which, years later, was to be the fate of her great-grandson, Lucien. But my mother was concerned for me; for my well-being; for my sanity.

"God doesn't talk through rocks," Mom would insist. "If you want to learn what God has to say, read the Bible like a good, sensible girl!"

Yes, Mom always wanted me to read from her old Bible. Now that she is no longer a part of my physical world perhaps I will respond to her often repeated request. Perhaps reading her Bible will help me to feel close to her just as listening to God through my rock beneath the Hummingtree keeps me close to my father.

Dad died when I was just a child. I am blessed that God allowed Mom to share forty-eight years of my journey on His good earth.

"The Lord giveth; the Lord taketh away." I'm sure Mom would share the quotation from the book of

Job if she were here right now. My mother was a religious woman. She liked to read her Bible and she was proud of her ability to quote verses verbatim from it.

Yes, Mom liked to read and even more than that, she liked to sing. She liked to play the old organ as she sang her favourite traditional hymns.

"Come play with me," she encouraged. "Come sing with me!"

And now I remember that as a child I would sit beside my mother on the old organ bench. I was not a good singer like my mother but I would do my best to harmonize my alto with her soft soprano as we sang songs like *Abide With Me* or *Just a Closer Walk With Thee.*

But this day I've lost my tongue. I cannot speak. My emotions fight to survive in my stomach

which is like a pretzel. It certainly feels like it is all tied
up in knots. My emotions are bound. Their need to rise
up to find my voice soon vanishes in the numbing
silence. Grief over-shadows the joy of new birth. Fear
buries my feelings alive.

*I am a grandmother now. My daughter Carol
brightened the world when she introduced Lucien, with
the corn silk hair and baby blue eyes into my life this
bright early morning.*

I wanted to celebrate!

*How could I, with any conscience, celebrate my
grandson's birth while I mourned the death of my
beautiful, dear mother?*

*That afternoon I felt alone in my grief. I wanted
to cry but the tears had solidified and become a part of
the mixture that sat like concrete in the pit of my
stomach.*

That was the weight I carried on my shoulders
as I left my old house.

What do I do? Where do I go?

I stood on the back deck. Fingers pointing
toward the back of my slippered heels, I sat my freckled
hands upon my wide hips. They must be freckles.
Surely I was too young then to have age spots. My
eyes surveyed the garden. It was a mild autumn and the
Potentillas were still in flower. I had already cut back

most of the flowers and bushes in case of an early northern winter.

The chipmunk scampers across the top of the garden wall. The deer have stayed away from my potted Dahlia plants. The black bears have not been so considerate. They have had a field day in the raspberry bushes down at the bottom of the yard. I caught only a glimpse of a foraging bear a couple of times. Most of their adventures in my garden take place in the dark of night. Even though the berries are long gone the bears, for their own reasons, enjoy playing in my backyard.

Winter was my friend when I was a child. In my early years I never felt the cold; never shied away from the whistling wind that whipped my cheeks making them ruddy and redder than my auburn hair. As a child I loved to toboggan down the hill, skate on the ice or lay down on the white earth, sliding my arms and legs back and forth, back and forth, creating snow angels but now, in my old age, I no longer want to befriend the harshness of Canadian winter.

I am grateful that the black bear feels the same way and spends the coldest months of the year in hibernation. I don't like to admit that I am afraid of the black bear but they are predatory. It is common fact that to them everything is food. *How can I know with certainty they wouldn't find me a tasty treat?*

What I really wanted that day was the opportunity to sit on God's good earth beneath my Hummingtree. I wanted to hear what I needed to hear.

I wanted to say what I needed to say. I wanted to lean on my yellow quartz rock and allow myself to contemplate the juxtaposition of my grandson's joyful birth and the overwhelming sense of loss that enveloped me now that Mother was gone.

Knowing that Mom was at peace and resting with God in her room in His heavenly palace did not erase the pain of loss that left me feeling sad, needy and alone. Knowing that my grandson was alive, healthy and an important part of my future; knowing that his arrival announced my entrance into grandmotherhood was something I wanted to celebrate. I wanted to experience the happiness that such an event should provide.

I was betwixt and between; neither here nor there. I was an emotional mess.

From my vantage point on the back deck I could clearly see my bench as it sat all alone beside the rock beneath the lilac tree which had long ago lost its purple blossoms. It was a simple matter to descend the deck's stairs onto the faded red brick patio, cross the yard and further descend to the bottom level of the yard where my bench was resting on the grass waiting for me. All I needed to do was to follow the concrete stairway. *Then all I could think of was Dorothy and The Wizard of Oz. My mind found its voice and started to sing. "Follow the yellow brick road; follow the yellow brick road; follow, follow, follow, follow"* – Follow the concrete stairway. Follow the stairway down to my bench.

Am I losing my mind?

My feet were stuck to the deck.

Long ago I had learned from my father that Native North Americans considered the black bear a totem of strength; an image of a spirit guide. *Daddy would never be afraid of the black bear,* the child within me chided.

Fear was winning the inner battle that raged. Fear pinned the soles of my feet to the pressure-treated wood while my legs shook causing my knees to knock together. This jiggling jostle caused my pretzel-knotted stomach to bounce like an Indian rubber ball that hit my bladder and told me I had better get back inside the house. I had to pee.

Once indoors I breathed a sigh of relief and resolved to stay there. As much as I wanted to be outside to sit beneath my Hummingtree I decided that, instead, I would sit in the safety of the arms of my cozy, blue, living-room lazy-boy lounger.

But once I was finally sitting in the comfort of the soft, warm chair I felt far from peaceful as I thought of all that lay ahead. There were practical matters to be dealt with. They would be demanding my attention. I was an only child. I had no siblings to help me with all that needed to be done. I would need to attend to the funeral ritual. I had to pay bills and keep track of receipts.

Who was there to help me? Friends had faded away over time. Many who earlier had played a large part in my life were now dead or moved away. There was no one I could call upon. My parents were gone. My husband, Jerry, never returned after that dreadful day when the heavens opened and emptied themselves through the roof of the old house we had lived in. The youngest girl, Sandi, was away at college and Carol, my elder daughter was in hospital. She carried my first grandchild in her welcoming arms.

My first child had given birth to a child of her own. My grieving heart would not allow me to celebrate my entrance into the brand-new world of grandmotherness. My sense of aloneness was painful. I thought I should not be alone yet I was unaware of anyone who could, by their presence, fill the hole; dull the knife that kept stabbing within me.

Maybe I could have called my neighbour, Emma, but she was already convinced that I was just the crazy lady who talked to God in a rock. I knew she was a good woman but I also knew she couldn't give me the help I desperately needed. No, indeed, there was no one to help me.

Sitting there in my living-room I tried to meditate. I closed my eyes and took a deep breath. *Focus on your breathing. Breathe in. Breathe out. Let your worries and your fears evaporate as though they had never existed. Breathe in. Breathe .....* It was a useless exercise. I could not relax. I opened my eyes and stared at the shelf on the opposite wall.

[112]

That's when I noticed the translucent, gleaming, glass angel smiling down upon my dismay and my discomfort. How often over the years had I dusted this glass angel in my automatic, routine way without really looking at it? How often had I held it in my hand feeling nothing but resentment because I did not want to clean it? I did not enjoy the necessary task of dusting, dusting and more dusting that was for years an integral part of my life as I lived alone in this old house. There was much about my life that I resented yet it was seldom that I was willing to acknowledge that resentment was, indeed, a part of my emotional being.

Resentment was something that I kept stored in a large, tight container in the basement of my soul. I kept it as deeply buried as my mother had hidden my father's journal. To acknowledge this resentment today, of all days, when I needed to be grieving the death of my mother; when I needed to be celebrating the birth of my grandchild, was not something I wanted to do.

I was becoming locked in memory with my feet stuck in the past. Then I remembered an old saying taught to me long ago by a friend. *If you have one foot in the past and the other in the future, you won't have a leg to stand on in the present.*

And there I was; sitting in my lazy-boy chair unable to stand up and face the truth of my situation because I was truly in an emotional limbo with no leg to stand upon.

[113]

Memory kept knocking on the door of my mind. I refused to answer. I refused to open the door. I felt frozen. I just wanted to go to sleep. But memory kept up its determined knock, knock, knock.

I grew tired of being stubborn and resistant. I grew plain old-fashioned tired. I gave up and I gave in. The next time memory knocked I listened as it talked to me. Upon listening I became vulnerable and it was my vulnerability that responded. *Yes, I remember the day my mother gifted me with the beautiful, gleaming, glass angel of protection.*

Once I acknowledged the memory I was able to pull myself out of the old chair. With two legs to stand on I walked across the floor of the living-room and stretched my needful arm up just far enough to allow my empty fingers to wrap around the angel's shiny, smooth body.

Touching the angel lifted my heart. Today this act of touch was very different from days past when I would quickly grab it just long enough to wrap the dusting cloth around it.

Today this act of touch enabled me to feel my mother's love as it flowed through me. It was as though she were saying, "Didn't I always take good care of you? Wasn't I always a good mother? Just because I've gone to my heavenly home does not mean I won't continue to be with you. My child, don't you know I will be with you always?"

The tangled knot in my stomach began to unravel as I felt my mother's loving protection flow through the angel and throughout my body until I was filled with love from head to toe.

At last I was ready. I was more than ready to do what I knew had to be done.

Once more I left the house and stepped onto the back deck. Bears beware! The war that had raged in my stomach and in my mind was over at last. Faith easily defeated fear.

Glass angel in hand I strode with purpose across the patio and down the concrete steps. My mother's angel in my grasp, my eyes on my father's yellow quartz rock, I was one with my parents as I sat down on the garden bench beneath my Lilac Hummingtree.

Yes, it was true that throughout most of my childhood my parents had been separated. My mother stayed home and did her best to raise me on her own while my father left to work as a trapper in Canada's far north country. But in this moment as I sat on the bench in my back yard my parents were together with me and we were family.

With these thoughts in mind, I stood my mother's angel atop my father's yellow quartz rock. This symbolic action assured me that my parents were reunited. This union also helped me to feel that both my parents were with me in spirit.

I sat on the garden bench and for several minutes I focused my gaze on the angel that rested atop my yellow quartz rock. Then leaning forward and slightly to the side so that I could have my voice in line with the hole in the rock, in a whisper, I asked, "Hello God, it's me, Ellen. Are you there?"

The yellow quartz rock soon began to hum. I sat back on the bench, closed my eyes, and as had happened for me often throughout my life, the humming became a tremor in the soles of my feet. As it moved through the rock to the trunk of the tree, it also moved through my legs to the trunk of my body. Soon the branches of the tree were a humming umbrella.

I felt the presence of my mother, of my father and I felt the powerful presence of God. I was no longer feeling abandoned or alone. No words were exchanged. They were not needed.

And then something unusual occurred.

In peaceful harmony I heard, along with the humming, a rustling sound. I felt great solid warmth emanating from the spot where the angel rested on the rock. I felt the brush of angel hair against my arm. I could smell an unusual fragrance; not the most pleasant odor but one that seemed foreign, other-worldly. With my eyes closed I could see nothing. Then I heard another strange sound. It was as I imagined glass would sound if it were crunched.

I had to open my eyes.

When I did, I saw the black bear rambling off away from me, over the fence, and into the bush behind my backyard. I looked at my yellow quartz rock. Its hum was much quieter now. I looked for my angel of protection. It was gone.

I know it's true that black bears will eat anything. Black bears will even eat glass. No, the bear did not harm me but he stole my angel. He not only stole it, but also he swallowed my angel before he turned his back on me. I was grateful that the black bear had been prepared to leave me alone as I sat on my garden bench in quiet meditation.

At last I was able to cry. As the tears flowed like a river across my cheeks and dripped like a tap from my chin to my dress, I prayed, "What should I do, God? The bear has eaten my angel. There is no way on your good earth that I can ever retrieve it."

To hear God's response more clearly I leaned over and held my right ear very close to the hole in the yellow, quartz rock.

"Are you certain you can never retrieve it, Ellen?"

"I'm very sure, Lord."

"Exactly what is it that the bear has stolen from you?"

"He has stolen the beautiful, translucent, glass angel my mother gave to me many years ago," I replied.

"Was the angel just a shiny piece of glass, Ellen?"

"Of course not, Lord. The angel carried my mother's love and protection. When she gave me the angel it was like she was promising she would always watch over me."

"Aah, I see," said my Lord. *"So the bear has stolen your mother's promise and protection, Ellen?"*

"Oh, no, Lord," the bear could never take that away from me. Nothing and no one can ever take my mother's love away from me. I don't mean to be rude but not even you, God."

"Nor would I ever want to take a mother's love from her child. Just as I would never take my love away from any of my children, including you, dear Ellen."

"I know that, Lord, and I am grateful. But how will I retrieve my glass angel?"

[118]

"Your mother tells me she has left you her Bible, Ellen. She wants you to read it. If you go to the book of Corinthians you will read words sort of like, 'If I speak with the tongues of men and of angels but have not love I have become as sounding brass or a tinkling cymbal' ....or maybe even as the sound of crunching glass, Ellen?"

I was astonished and filled with gratitude.

"Thank you for helping me to retrieve my mother's angel. You are so very right as always, Lord. My mother's gift to me was not just a piece of noisily chewed glass. The angel was filled with her devotion. Maybe that old, black bear did eat the glass but he could not devour all the love it contained because my mother's love, like yours, is endless."

"Celebrate life, Ellen; that of your mother and that of your grandchild."

Since that conversation I've swallowed twenty years but I still get a lump in my throat when I remember that October day. Have I spent my time in celebration?

I can say I've had my moments.

SEVEN

SEVEN:

The Carpenter:

As I sit here in the blue lazy-boy chair in my comfortable living-room and gaze with wonder at the beautiful, honey golden wood sculpture I remember the carpenter who created the masterpiece that is now at home on my fireplace mantel. I know I am truly blessed to have this work of art in my possession. Not too many know that there was a time, many years ago when I was single again, that I could have also been blessed to accept this good man's proposal of marriage.

To the best of my poor memory I want to now share with you what my carpenter friend, William, told me about his experience of shaping this smooth as corn silk creation. I was not sitting beneath the Hummingtree when my ears were caressed by the sensual sound of his voice. No, indeed. In fact William sat across from me in a chair in this very room. Little has changed over the years in this tired living-room. It still contains the same old sofa, same old lazy-boy chair, same old coffee table and same old lamps that now help me to shed light on the loving memories of my carpenter.

As he told the tale, William's words were as effortless and as persuasive as a lover's hands. They are words I will never forget. I remember he began by speaking my name. The gentleness of his soft voice

[121]

made an ordinary name such as mine sound very special and from this precious beginning there flowed a conversation between us.

I don't remember the conversation verbatim but I will do my best to share with you the substance of it. Once you have heard my telling of his story then I am quite certain you will understand the significance and importance to me of the beautiful wood sculpture that graces the top of my old living-room fireplace mantel.

Ellen, I want you to accept this gift, William said. *It's something I've had kicking around the house for some time now. It's almost like it is an extension of myself, if you will, and though it gives me pleasure to gift you I confess that in many ways it pains me to see it go.*

The sculptured wood was simply beautiful; almost sensual to the touch with smooth effortless curves and its sweet honey shade almost matched the dear man's complexion. "I couldn't possibly accept such a gift, William," I replied.

You must, my dear Ellen. It pleases me beyond measure to be a witness to the pleasure reflected in your eyes when you look at the piece. Please accept it. He smiled before he added, *I insist.*

Then I insist on paying you, William.

No, I don't want any money for it, Ellen.

But William .....

[122]

Shh! I don't want to hear another word about payments or receipts or any of that kind of stuff. I want you to please accept this humble offering as a gift.

He passed the wooden sculpture to me. I cradled it in my arms and said, "Thank you, William. I will treasure it forever, my dear friend."

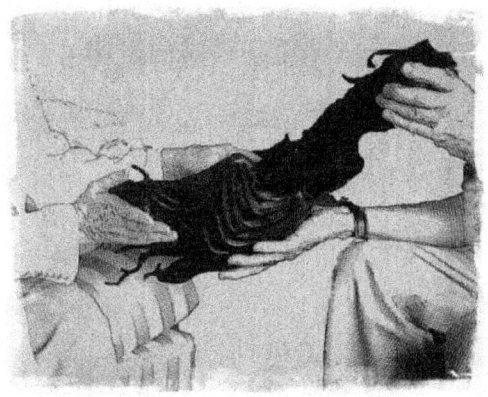

I know you will just as I have done since the first time I lay my eyes upon it, Ellen. The way I see it, this piece of wood was a gift that I stumbled across and I am not a man who goes through life taking a lot of false steps.

William had a quiet confidence that I almost envied. I had no doubt that he was speaking the truth. "However did you find it?" I asked.

He began to speak and I sat enthralled on the sofa chair while I listened to dear William tell me his story about the unexpected arrival of this very precious sculpture into his life.

Ellen, he said, *I was taking my time as I walked home from the worship service at the Methodist Church one Sunday morning about twelve years ago. I guess you could say I was kind of lost in thought as I considered the words old Reverend Wilson had preached. In that morning's service he had sermonized about the years Jesus worked with his father, Joseph, who was a carpenter. Reverend Wilson was asking the question, "Was Jesus a carpenter?"*

I knew I shouldn't but I couldn't resist the urge to interrupt William's story. I said, "Everyone knows that Jesus was a carpenter, William. Why on earth would Reverend Wilson ask such a ridiculous question?"

Well, according to Reverend Wilson's understanding there was no such evidence to prove that Jesus was a carpenter. This is what he said, Ellen. He said we know his father, Joseph, was a carpenter and from the cultural times it may be safe to assume that Jesus took up the trade until his ministry began. That's what the good Reverend said. And, Ellen, did you know that Jesus' ministry didn't even get started until he was thirty years old?

"Yes, I know that," I replied. "I have to admit that at least some of my good mother's teachings have stayed with me. I suppose that in his earlier years Jesus needed to make a living just like everyone else. Some things never change. And I don't doubt for a minute that he worked as a carpenter just like you, William.

Come to think of it, we don't hear much about his early education or his career, do we?"

No, we don't, Ellen. That is a fact.

"So many years of his life we know next to nothing about. Maybe he apprenticed with his dad? That would seem logical, wouldn't it, William?

Yes, Ellen, but keep in mind Reverend Wilson doesn't always hold with a lot of logic when he is preparing his Sunday morning sermons.

"Well, William, I am not so well acquainted with Reverend Wilson to feel able to comment on that statement. But it just stands to reason that Jesus, like most young boys in those long ago times, would have apprenticed with his carpenter father. Since he didn't start his real important work until he was thirty I guess today we would call him a late bloomer," I laughed.

But then the disappointed look on William's face made me re-think and regret my choice of words. I knew before his disappointed, questioning response that I had injured his feelings.

Even you, Ellen, do not believe his work as a carpenter was important? You believe his real important work didn't start until he was thirty? William asked me.

I felt bad. I hadn't meant to hurt his feelings.

[125]

"What I meant to say, William," I responded, "is that I was aware that the ministry of Jesus didn't start until he was thirty. I'm sorry if my clumsy choice of words upset you. Of course the work of a carpenter is very important. Why, if there were no carpenters we wouldn't be living in fine houses, would we? We would still be living in teepees like my Daddy did when he lived up north with the Cree Indians."

Don't apologize, Ellen. I'm just being overly-sensitive, he replied. *And, yes, what you say is true. Jesus did not start his ministry until he was thirty. At least that is what we have been taught. And that morning in church when Reverend Wilson opened up the Bible he quoted from the book of Mark, Chapter six, Verse three. Now I may not be one hundred percent in my accuracy but, as I recall, the words he read were, "Is not this the carpenter, the son of Mary and brother of James, Judas and Simon, and are not his sisters here with us? And they took offence at him."*

I could see that once he finished speaking William's lips were locked in a grimace. With frustration pushing his strong arms up over his head he waved his open-hands, fingers flailing, into the air as he resumed talking.

I didn't understand. I knew I was talking too much and interfering with his telling of the story but I had to ask, "William, why have the Reverend's words upset you in this way?"

I know I shouldn't get mad, Ellen, but you just heard me read that they took offence at Him. Why would people take offence at such an event? Did they think that because they knew Jesus just as a carpenter or son of a carpenter that he should not be allowed to preach in the synagogue in Nazareth? I mean why wouldn't a carpenter have as much right as anyone else to give voice to his thoughts in order to share his message with others? I mean what's wrong with being a carpenter?

There is nothing wrong with being a carpenter, I assured my dear friend. "My goodness, William, you are a wonderful carpenter. Everyone knows you are the best in town."

I'm proud to be a carpenter and why shouldn't I be?

"Of course you should feel proud. I'm very proud of you too."

Thank you but as you can see, Ellen, I have a lot of questions that I would love to have satisfied by some easy to understand answers.

I didn't really see or understand his distress at all. In fact I felt quite useless and inadequate given the situation I found myself in. I was out of my depth in this conversation. I am being generous when I say my knowledge of the Bible was limited. Maybe I should have read more when my dear mother urged me to do so throughout my own early childhood years. But I didn't and now as William poured out his story to me I could think of nothing intelligent to say. I could only sit there and listen.

Now that time has passed and I allow myself to look back into the past and remember this day I can only say I'm grateful that I took the time to listen to his telling of the story that day.

"Please tell me more. I'll try not to interrupt so often. Go on with your story, William," I said.

Okay, Ellen, he said. *To get back to my story about the day I stumbled across this piece of wood, these thoughts I've expressed to you were what I had in my mind as I made my way home from church that morning. I was feeling angry and I guess I wasn't really looking where I was going because one minute I was walking past somebody's front verandah that held a big pot filled with a dahlia plant and the next minute I was laying on the ground expecting angels to gather round to sing Abide With Me.*

Ellen, what I mean to say is, I had blacked out and thought I'd died.

Oh, my!

When I opened my eyes I was lying on the ground and staring at a plain piece of wood. Part of a tree's roots it was growing from the earth but instead of reaching for the sky I could see that the roots spread outward. Somehow it remained inside of itself. Its shape was as crooked as my arthritic hands.

[128]

"Arthritis is a terrible disease," I said.

And here I was interrupting his story again. I couldn't seem to keep quiet and just sit there and listen even though I knew that was exactly what William not only wanted but also needed.

"I'm sorry for the terrible pain the arthritis causes you, William. I wish there were a cure available," I sympathized. "As you know I suffer from the dread disease too.

I've had arthritis in my hands for so many years it's just something I live with; not something I ever hope to change, Ellen. But that morning, after giving thanks to God that I was still alive, I reached out and caressed that piece of tree root. Believe it or not, my hands were warmed by the touch of that wood. My hands were comforted and the consistent, chronic pain vanished.

"Oh, my! Just like that? That's a miracle!"

Yes, Ellen, a miracle. It was like Jesus, the master carpenter himself, was holding my hands. I believed it was a miracle.

"Your story lifts me up so high, William. I believe in miracles."

As do I, but when I pulled my hands away from that piece of wood the arthritic pain returned.

"Oh, dear." I asked, "What's a man to do? You can't spend your entire life walking around with a piece of wood in your hands now, can you, William? Oh, I guess that is a very stupid thing to say. I'm so sorry for my persistent interruptions and, more than that, I'm sorry for the pain the arthritis gives you."

No need for pity, Ellen, and, of course, you are correct. As much as I wanted to be healed, I knew I couldn't spend my life carrying around a piece of wood in my hands. But at the same time without truly knowing why and without having any idea what I would do with it, I made a decision. That is exactly when I knew without a doubt that I had to take that piece of wood home with me.

Somehow I felt it was no coincidence that I had tripped over those tree roots. Since my mind had been so deeply focused on Reverend Wilson's words about Jesus that morning, I felt that He had guided my steps and caused me to black out and fall. How else could I possibly have learned of the healing power that was flowing through that piece of wood, Ellen?

"William, I am speechless!" I exclaimed but of course I wasn't speechless at all or I would learn once and for all to keep my blasted mouth shut and allow this dear man to get on with his story.

Ellen, I took that plain old piece of wood home with me that day and it was something that I worked on for a very long time. I used sand paper and carpenter's tools to round the edges. As the wood began to take

[130]

shape I felt as though I were giving birth to something that was a part of me yet much greater than myself. I wondered if this was how God felt when he created this planet. I reached way down deep inside of myself and found a design that made a natural pairing with the wood. It was simple. It felt natural. In that holy instant of creation I felt one with the Master Carpenter.

At first I didn't like the streaks that showed through the wood and no matter how hard I rubbed, no matter how much I willed them to be gone once and for all, those streaks were there to stay. That is when I learned to love the streaks.

Caressing the sculpture I agreed. "I love the streaks too, William. In my opinion I believe they give the piece character and personality."

Yes, Ellen, and the streaks were a teacher. From them I learned a lot about myself. That is when I realized that the streaks in me; the selfish streak, the mean streak, the streaks of kindness, were an integral part of the man I am. And I learned that day that, sure, I could round my own sharp corners and I could try to erase the not-so-nice mannerisms but no matter how hard I worked at doing those things, whether I met with success or not, throughout the entire process God loves me just as I am; the good, the bad and the ugly. This awareness made me feel very close to the Master Carpenter.

"Your story touches my heart. It makes me want to cry, William."

As long as they are happy tears, Ellen, because it was then that I began to see a bigger picture forming in my reawakened vision. That's when I knew that this healing piece of wood was going to be transformed.

"Oh, my, it is, indeed, a miracle!"

At first I felt hesitant to use the nails. God knows I did not want to ruin the piece by splitting the wood. When I began with the hammer the wood did splinter but just a little. Fortunately it did not split. When it splintered I wanted to cry but through my tears, Ellen, I was able to see that the splinter was not unpleasant to the eye. It was, in fact, interesting and that was when I began to see that this old piece of wood really had some potential to be a valuable work of art. As long as I didn't mess it up, that is.

"And you certainly didn't do that. It is beautiful exactly as it is, William."

Strangely enough when that nail splintered the wood a little it reminded me of a time when I was just a young lad. I'd been collecting odd bits and pieces of wood with the hope that I could construct a wagon for myself; one in which I hoped to pull my toys or special rocks that I found or even my mother's groceries on our Saturday morning walks home from the supermarket. I really wanted that wagon and I did a pretty decent job with its construction. I had it all put together with the wheels on and everything. All that remained to be done was to put the handle onto the front of it so that I could pull it and steer it.

As I was hitting the nail to complete the job the wood at the front of the wagon splintered. I had no choice but to move the handle over but that, in my opinion, looked kind of stupid. So then I had an idea that if I put two handles on my wagon; one on either side of the front panel, and if I had those two handles come together to meet on the open end then I would have a wagon that was unique and different from all the other boys in the neighbourhood.

"What a clever idea! Did you do that?"

Yes, Ellen, I did just that. And that wagon was the envy of all the other kids in the neighbourhood. If I had not splintered the wood I would have had an ordinary handle on my wagon that was no better, no worse than any other wagon in the district.

I recalled this memory of the wagon when I splintered the plain piece of wood and that recollection set the stage to turn the wood into something of beauty; something a person would want to own.

Overwhelmed, I asked, "And you are giving it to me? You really want me to keep it? Oh, my! William, I am so very honoured to own this beautiful work."

Thank you, Ellen. I think you will understand when I say that this memory also made me realize that the more often I am scarred by life and the more often my emotions are splintered then, as a consequence, the more strength and endurance I develop. I thought, you

[133]

know, it is in my imperfection that I recognize perfection. I mean, Ellen, nobody is perfect, right?

"Oh, I know I am very far from perfect, William." I smiled.

But, don't you see, Ellen? By knowing this we learn to be tolerant and accepting of the imperfections in others and we hope that others will give us the same respect and love in return.

I learned a lot about life working with this healing piece of wood.

I felt as though the wood had surrendered itself to me. And that made me think again of Reverend Wilson and I began to have some greater understanding of what he was talking about when he said we needed to surrender ourselves to God.

"I always feel I should never give up, William. Isn't surrendering an act of weakness?"

The act of surrendering is not an act of weakness, Ellen. No, indeed it is not. When that wood allowed me to do with it what I needed to do in order to create a work of art that piece of wood grew in strength, in beauty and its healing powers increased.

And it's funny how my thoughts went from one thing to another as I smeared some glue here and there to keep the creation together as I intended it to be. Because out of the blue came thoughts of the carpenter, Jesus, and I remembered again some words Reverend

Wilson had said. He was quoting from the Bible again. I think this time it was from Luke where it says, "And Jesus grew in wisdom and in stature and in favour with God and men."

It seemed to me that, just like the wood, the more Jesus had to go through; the more He suffered and endured; the stronger, the wiser and the more appreciated He became. Sometimes we need to be lost before there can be any thought of being found, Ellen.

"Oh, I see just what you mean, William, though I confess I've never thought of it that way before."

I hadn't either, Ellen, until that morning. I mean according to Reverend Wilson, Jesus grew up among a people who were subjected to the dominance of a foreign oppressor in a conquered province of the Roman Empire; in the darkest district of Palestine. He grew up in poverty, in manual labour, and in the obscurity of his father's carpenter shop. Yet, Ellen, here we are, thousands of years later, acquainted with this Jesus who was well acquainted with sorrow. In spite of His own suffering He has brought joy and peace into the lives of so many.

And thinking of Jesus and all that he had to go through made me realize that even me; even me, a simple carpenter, can create change. By transforming a plain piece of wood into a valuable work of art I am creating the potential of transformation within any and all who view the finished piece.

"It's true you are an amazing talented carpenter, William."

I hope this doesn't sound like I'm boasting, Ellen. I mean when I was working with this piece of wood, I honestly do not believe I was experiencing illusions of grandeur. I do believe that I was learning valuable lessons that have helped to make me a better carpenter but, more important, a better man.

As I worked and began to shape this piece of wood into what it is today I could not help but smile. While I worked, I would dream. I would dream of a better world. I would realize that there are no accidents; that there is a reason and a purpose in all things. And I learned that we would accept these things as truths if we were not afraid to just let go and let God guide us on our journey throughout this life.

"What wonderful lessons you have learned from a simple piece of wood, William. Thank you for sharing your story."

It's my pleasure to share it with you, Ellen. You see, since finishing this piece I kept it in my own home for many years. I kept it until one day just last week when I had an epiphany.

"An epiphany?" I hated to show my ignorance but I decided it would be even more ignorant to pretend I understood what he was saying when, in fact, I did not. I had to ask, "William, what is an epiphany?"

It's like a sudden realization about the true meaning of something, Ellen. Sort of like seeing the big picture if you know what I mean.

"Seeing the big picture? Yes, I do understand that, William."

Now, I come to the hard part of what I want to say to you, today Ellen. Please don't take this the wrong way, but I've heard around town that you claim to talk to God through a rock in your backyard. Is this true, Ellen?

"Yes, William. At the risk of sounding like a crazy lady I confess that is absolutely true."

And you claim to have a special relationship with God that you share through the rock under what you label the Hummingtree in your backyard?

"Hmm, word does get around this small gossipy town, doesn't it William? Where rumors flourish an ounce of truth exists. Oh, my," I cried. "I do confess that what you say is true. And I suppose, like lots of the folks around here, you think I'm crazy too, William?

Don't get angry, but yes, Ellen, before I stumbled over this piece of wood I did think you were, shall I say somewhat unusual; or should I say eccentric and certainly different. But since my epiphany I have had to take the time to look at how I view the world and all God's creatures which inhabit this fragile place.

[137]

And now I can, with absolute frankness, say that, no, Ellen, I don't think you are crazy in the least.

On the contrary in fact. When I heard the stories about you, I knew you were the person I wanted to gift with this wooden creation.

You see, Ellen, the divine manifestation I am talking about that took place just last week was a voice that spoke to me. I will tell this to you, Ellen, but to no one else. I believe none but you will understand. You see, the voice was barely above a whisper which reached my ears as I caressed the healing wood with my hands. Would you like to know what the voice said, Ellen?

"Oh, yes please, William."

Then I will tell you what the voice said. It said, "Give this piece of wood to Ellen. You have already learned its lessons and by sharing this gift with her, she will also grow in wisdom and she will, in turn, share her learning with her family."

"Oh, my goodness. Whose voice were you hearing, William?"

In my heart I believed it was the voice of God, Ellen.

"Oh, my dear William. How wonderful! If God can speak to me through my yellow quartz rock then there is no doubt in my mind that He spoke to you through this beautiful piece of wood."

*I knew you would understand, Ellen. The way I
see it, it's like it was all meant to be. Who, but you,
would not consider me a crazy man who talks to wood?
You are the only person I know who will truly
understand my knowing that God has talked to me and
healed me through this piece of wood.*

Ellen, I want you to accept this gift.

And, of course I did. I felt honoured and I
accepted William's gift. I accepted his generosity and
his love. But, no, it was not on that day but when it
came I did not accept his proposal of marriage.

Now these many years later I have learned that
William passed away last month. I miss him and I will
always remember him. He was a good man with a
good, kind, caring heart. Just like his Lord, he was a
creator. He was the carpenter who, just like God,
accepted me for who I am.

It is William who taught me that transformation
can and does take place in this tired old world. And
perhaps the greatest transformation is within a person's
thoughts. William taught me that thoughts are not
intangibles. Thoughts are very real and powerful
things.

When I leave this life on earth I will be leaving
behind so many different parts of myself; parts of me
that I have inserted into my stories; parts of me that
are alive in my children and my grandchildren. I will
leave behind so many photo albums filled with pictures

[139]

of my life's adventure; poems I have written, people I have loved and memories I have savoured.

I'm equally certain many unfinished things will be left behind because even though I know timelessness exists there never seems to be enough time for me to get it all done. My loving memory of William, the carpenter, is something I will need to leave behind along with his inspirational wooden sculpture that is now mine to treasure.

As I sit here in my living-room and gaze with wonder at the beautiful, honey golden wood sculpture I remember the carpenter who created this masterpiece. I am blessed to have this work of art in my possession and there it will remain until the day arrives when this too shall be left behind.

Perhaps God will direct my steps to someone with whom I can share my story about William; about this work of art and about the miracle of transformation. For now I share these memories and these thoughts in my writing not even knowing if the words will be read. But I simply trust that life in its unfoldment will be what it is meant to be. I was blessed to know William. He taught me that thoughts are very tangible and important things.

I miss him. I love him still and I will always remember the carpenter who created the masterpiece that is now at home on my fireplace mantel. He created something even greater within my heart and this special something I will treasure forever.

EIGHT

EIGHT:

Abundance:

After Jerry left me, William was not the only man who shared more than a casual interest in me and my life. Jethro also loved me. I must confess my relationship with Jethro is another story altogether. By the time he came into my life I had already become what the so-called experts liked to call the proverbial empty-nester.

Both daughters, Sandi and Carol, had left home. They each were focused on a career and they were making their own way in the world.

It had been years since Jerry abandoned his family and, though it wasn't easy, I had finally accepted that he was not coming back to me; to our marriage. I was alone in the world and I felt lonely. The forty-nine year old woman staring back at me in the mirror was a caricature of the practical, purposeful person I used to be. I swear there were times that I could barely contain the urge to slap her face.

Joy had turned its back on me. And you can take my word for it; worrying about money was no pleasure either but, knowing this, I could not seem to make myself stop doing it. I jumped every time the phone rang and maybe it was a good thing I didn't get a lot of company because at that juncture of my life I was scared to answer my own front door.

[142]

The power has been turned off in my house but that was okay. I could live without electricity. I had even learned to like the cozy, sheltering warmth of the old oil lamp. Indeed, the shadows dancing on the walls in the dark of evening had become my only source of entertainment. As for cooking, I was doing my best with the old backyard barbecue. I had no idea what I would do when the charcoal ran out. And I didn't even want to think about the whelp of winter on this beautiful, small town, summer day.

I thought of my mother and I could almost hear her voice saying, "This is another fine kettle of fish!"

Yes, a fine kettle, indeed. On this fine summer day I finish the dishes, dry my hands on my apron, and decide that what I need to do is to get out of the house. Maybe the morning's fresh, fragrant air will force the worry whirlpool out of my swollen head. I decide that I will take a walk on the trail through the woods behind the house.

I've almost reached the garden gate when the yellow quartz boulder beneath the Hummingtree whispers my name. I can hear it calling, *Ellen, come rest a while.*

I ignore the invitation. For the past many weeks I've spent time sitting on God's good earth beneath the Hummingtree. I've sat cross-legged on the soft, green grass and, in my usual way, I have leaned over the yellow quartz rock and shared my money problems

[143]

with God. And each time His promise reached my ears; *Abundance is on its way.*

At first because I wanted to believe I would simply reply, "Thank you, God." But as time went by and my financial situation did nothing to improve itself I began to doubt His promise.

Abundance is on its way, the Good Lord repeated when I continued to beg for help.

It's taking its own sweet time getting here, I answered. And after several weeks of receiving this repetitive pledge with no money arriving on my doorstep I was fast losing faith.

Ellen, come rest a while, the voice persisted that morning.

Feeling mean and miserable, I leaned over and picked up a pebble. **I** tossed it as hard as I could and watched with satisfaction when it bounced off the yellow quartz rock onto the grass.

I walk to the garden gate, open it, and begin my trek through the woods. There are few animals about this morning. I spot a couple of black squirrels scurrying along the branch of a Maple. I hear the crows cussing. I see a chipmunk turn and run at the sound of my approaching footsteps. No bears about this morning and for this I'm grateful as I allow my mind to enter the stillness.

I walk for almost an hour and by the time I'm home and have reached the garden gate I am no closer to a solution to my financial problems. Back inside the yard I glance over at my yellow quartz rock. Feeling dismayed and discouraged, I make my way across the crisp, green grass and settle myself on the soft earth beneath the Hummingtree.

I folded my legs beneath me and bowed my head to pray. *Silly fool, you're still wearing your apron*, I chide myself. With a sigh, I lean over the rock and whisper, *it's me again, Lord. Are you there? I'm sorry I threw the pebble. I didn't mean it. I hope you will forgive me and my impatience.*

I can feel the vibration massaging my feet and my legs as the humming makes its way up the trunk of the tree. I hold my ear close to the hole in the rock and soon the same old message reaches me once again, *Abundance is on its way, Ellen.*

Where's it coming from, Lord? And how much longer do I need to wait?

Patience is a virtue, Ellen. There are reasons for waiting.

That may be so, Lord, but I can't pay the bills with patience. It's money I'm needing.

There are reasons for waiting, Ellen.

I lift my weary body up from the ground and carry my impatience and my worry through the

[145]

backyard. My intention is to go back into the house where, for the thousandth time, I will scan the local newspaper's classified section in search of an opportunity to make some much needed money.

The welcoming, white, plastic lawn chair on the patio calls out to me and I allow myself to collapse into its old reliable comfort. *Who am I Kidding? I know without looking that there will be no jobs in the small town paper and certainly nothing for a no-skills female of forty-nine.*

Then the tears come. Self-pity makes itself at home in my heart while my head pounds with what threatens to be a migraine. That's when it happens. I nearly jump out of my skin at the sound of the deep, unfamiliar, masculine voice.

"Hello, I'm looking for Ellen Dawson. Would that be you?" he asked.

I look up to see a short, pot-bellied, bearded fellow with a knapsack on his back. He is standing at my backyard gate. His crooked smile and crinkled eyes peering out over the shaggy beard are not reminiscent of a bill collector but these days you never know the truth about people. I needed to make sure I wasn't in for more harassment.

"Who wants to know?" I asked.

"I want to know," he answered. "Folks in town told me I'd find Ellen Dawson at this address. Would that be you?"

"Why do you want to meet Ellen Dawson?" I ask, though the longer I look at him the more convinced I am that he is not a bill collector or someone who has come to turn off the water or put an eviction notice on my door.

The odd fellow's crooked smile grows bigger behind the beard and his voice can only be described as jovial when he speaks. "I'm obviously off to a very bad start. Let me start over," he says. "My name is Jethro. I'm a tourist in your lovely town. I planned to stay in the hotel but they sent me on my way because all the rooms are filled. Seems there's a big bicycle race happening this weekend. Never dawned on me I'd need a reservation and now I find myself with no place to stay."

"What's that got to do with me?" I ask.

"Like I said, I talked to some folks in town. They told me you just might be the one to help me out in this situation."

Bewildered, I simply sit in my plastic chair and stare at the old man.

His smile evaporates. "I'll be on my way then," he says. "Sorry to have troubled you, ma'am." He turns his back and, shoulders slumped, he is about to leave. *Good, let him go. I've got enough trouble and don't need more,* I think but what I say is, "Wait a minute. Don't go!"

As he turns toward me once again, I lift myself out of the chair, walk over to the backyard gate, hit the latch and pull the portal open. "Come in. I apologize for my rudeness. I'm Ellen Dawson."

"Why thank you, ma'am. Don't mind if I do."

"Take a seat here," I offer.

I watch with wonder as he removes the bulging backpack and places it squarely in front of him on the patio. With a big sigh of relief he lowers himself into the plastic chair and stretching his short, pudgy legs out he rests them atop the knapsack. "Thank you, ma'am."

I sit down across from him in the other white plastic lawn chair and take a closer look at the old fellow. He seems harmless enough and my initial fear is soon replaced by a comfortable curiosity. "Would you like a cold drink?" I ask.

[148]

"I don't want to put you to any trouble, ma'am, but a cold drink would go down well on this warm summer morning. I didn't realize how long a walk it was to get here from the town centre and these short legs of mine are a mite tired."

"It's no trouble."

Back inside the house I pull a colourful, flowered, metal serving tray out of the kitchen cupboard. On it I rest two tall glasses and a small plate. Habit makes me follow old patterns and I open the fridge door to remove the jug of warm iced tea. While I am filling the two glasses I stare out the window at the old man sitting in my lawn chair. Judging by his appearance I guess he won't say no to a good home-cooked meal. *He looks as lonesome as I feel.*

I don't have a whole lot of food in the house but I put a few Ritz crackers onto the plate and carry the tray out to the yard.

"Thank you, ma'am. It's not every day a person will offer kindness and comfort to a stranger."

"I don't like being called ma'am," I say. "Makes me feel old! My name is Ellen and that's what you can call me."

"Ellen," he replies, "my name is Jethro Tunkel. I am seventy-four years old and on my way to out-living myself. I made a decision last week when I said farewell to seventy-three and realized that I didn't feel like celebrating my 74th. I also realized that before I get too much older and die like most folks do, I want to see a little more of our beautiful country. So I left the bright lights, big city. Yes, I left Toronto and travelled north by Greyhound bus. I had to change buses three times and ended up in a little old school bus in order to get here but now I have arrived in your lovely town and the first thing I discover is that I have no place to lay my head."

"Jethro, why have you come to me? I'm not a hotel."

"Folks told me you were having a bit of a financial struggle out here on your own and it occurred to me that maybe we could help each other out a little."

"Hmm, folks! Folks in this town are never at a loss to find something to say about me!"

"Ellen, are you familiar with the music of a fellow named Bruce Tunkel? He shares my surname but no relation as far as I know."

"No, I've never heard of anybody named Tunkel. What kind of a funny name is that anyway?"

"Well, I guess it's not a very common name here in Canada. Tunkel is a Jewish name; at least I guess it is since it's my name and I just happen to be Jewish. And, Ellen, the lyrics to one of Bruce Tunkel's songs called *Beautiful World* come to mind as I look at you."

"You look at me and think of a beautiful world?"

"Don't know if I remember all the words but it goes something like this, *Did you say goodbye? Were you in love? Did you have faith in God up above? Looking for faith, searching for hope, searching for that something that helps us to cope.*"

I listen to the old man's soft, rough voice singing and the insightful words creep into my soul. Uninvited, unwelcome tears blanket my face. Before I know what is happening I feel like a total fool because I'm bawling my eyes out and laying my soul bare in front of this old stranger.

Jethro reaches out and lays his old, wrinkled hand upon my own and says, "It's okay, Ellen. It's okay."

I do my best to stop the water dripping from my eyes. And once I start sharing my sorrow with Jethro there is no stopping me. It is just like someone pulled a plug inside of me and out poured all my troubles; my fear about losing my home; my loneliness and my sense of downright uselessness.

Jethro smiles his crooked smile and says, "Ellen, I think I may have a solution to your problems. You've got a house and I need a home. You've got expenses and I've got some money. No, I'm not a wealthy man but I've got enough money to pay my way. I can pay you a fair amount for room and board.

[151]

And I may be an old man but I'm not totally over the hill yet. I can help you out around the house with chores if you will let me. Are you willing to take a chance on an old fellow who means you no harm?"

I look into the depths of his warm, brown eyes. I want to believe the safe feeling he is sending my way. "Are you an answer to my prayers, Jethro? I've been waiting for an answer for a very long time."

He surprises me with his response.

"There are always reasons for waiting, Ellen," he says with a chuckle.

I remember where I've heard those words before. "You're laughing at me!"

"Not laughing at you, Ellen. Thinking of myself as an answer to someone's prayer gives me a chuckle, that's all. And, you know, talking about waiting reminds me of another Jethro. Maybe you've heard of this one; Jethro Tull?"

"No, I've never met any Jethro before."

"Guess you can tell I like my music. This fellow I'm talking about sang a song called *Reasons for Waiting.* It goes something like this. *"Could it stop the sunrise hearing you weep? You're not seen. You're not heard but I stand by my word. Came a thousand miles just to catch you while you're smiling."*

[152]

Suddenly I am smiling. And no one is more surprised than me when I invite Jethro into my home and into my heart. Guess you could call him a tourist who over-stayed his visit. But I call him my answer to prayer.

He makes himself at home in what had been my daughter's bedroom. In return for his room and board Jethro is true to his word. He pays a reasonable rent every week. Soon I am able to answer the phone and not dread a knock on the door. Not only does he solve my financial problems, Jethro puts his love of gardening to work and helps me the entire summer with weeding and watering. He is a pleasure to know. I feel like a huge weight has been lifted from me and I can breathe freely once more.

One summer afternoon I am down at the bottom of the backyard, sitting on the soft earth beneath the Hummingtree. I am meditating and having a chat with the Lord through my yellow quartz rock when Jethro interrupts my reverie.

"What are you doing, Ellen?" he asks. "Are you talking to that rock?"

"I am," I say, enjoying his bewilderment.

"Wouldn't you rather talk to me, Ellen?"

I smile and answer, "What would you like to talk about then?"

"Oh, I don't know. Maybe I'll talk about myself." He lowered his pudgy body down onto the grass, wiggling a bit to make sure he'd found a most comfortable spot. Satisfied that he had, he turned to me and, out of the blue, he asked, "Do you know the meaning of my name, Ellen?"

"No, Jethro, I don't. The only Jethro I've ever heard of is the Biblical Jethro, father of Moses' wife, Zipporah, in the old testament."

"Well, Ellen, it is true that Jethro is an old name. It comes from the Hebrew name *Yitro* which is derived from the name *Yeter.*"

"That's very interesting, Jethro."

"Yep, and do you know what the name *Yeter* means, Ellen?"

"No, but I'm sure you're going to tell me, Jethro.

"Yes, ma'am. The name *Yeter* means *abundance.*"

Immediately I remember my conversation those long ago days when I was feeling despondent, depressed and devoid of hope. The good Lord had promised me, *Abundance is on its way.*

As I look into the old man's smiling eyes, I reach out from my spot on God's good earth and pat my yellow quartz rock. I know that Jethro is deaf to the humming that begins to make its way up the trunk of the tree but he is not blind to the light that fills my grateful eyes.

NINE

NINE:

The Hawkwood Retirement Resort:

When I first met Jason Knobest I wanted to wipe the self-serving smirk off his fat face. Smart ass know-it-all; he kept repeating the same lines over and over until I was pushed to the limit and ready to scream. I do not like pushy people!

"Trust me. It's for your own good, Ellen," he says. "We have your best interest at heart."

Ha! For my own good, indeed! What rug did you crawl out from under? But I guess I know what brought this trouble-maker to my door.

This is the result of what happens just because I had the flu. I caught the influenza two months ago. By now I am sure you know me well enough to understand that I am a person who never gets sick but, yes, I can't deny that I caught the darn flu and needed to spend a few days in bed. It all started with some sneezing; a bothersome head cold but somehow those germs travelled down and made themselves right at home in my chest where no amount of Vicks Vaporub could ease the pain produced by the annoying, persistent and horrible hacking cough.

My sensitive stomach didn't escape attack either and when I wasn't throwing up in the bathroom, I suffered with diarrhea. Though I couldn't find any humour in my sick situation there were moments when I remembered the old Laurel and Hardy shows and Laurel's famous words, "Another fine mess we're in, Ollie!" Yes, because of the flu, I was in a fine mess indeed!

I must say that both daughters, Carol and Sandi, were very good about coming to the house after work each day that I was ill to make sure I was okay and to see to it that I had everything I needed. They are good girls and I know they love me. For several days they took very good care of me.

At first their concern was foremost in their minds and they came together to see me. But as time passed they soon got tired of the daily visitations and they began to take turns. Carol came one day and Sandi the next. Neither daughter ever arrived empty-handed. They brought containers of home-made chicken soup and while in my home they brewed many pots of hot green tea. They fluffed up my pillows. The clatter of the dishes in the sink and the roar of the vacuum cleaner told me they were keeping the house tidy for me.

They even spent some precious time sitting on the chair beside my bed and talking with me. It wasn't often we shared conversation and for this reason I was able to appreciate that there was an upside to my miserable cold. Yes, my daughters were good girls; always had been and they were a blessing to me now when I was sick and needed their help.

Yes, I admit I was just a little slow in my recovery but I think that's natural given my age; not that I'm old, mind you, but at sixty-five I am getting up there. I am finally retired from the working world and with the pension cheques coming in on a regular basis now I don't feel pressured to earn any extra income. In fact, before I became ill, I was taking it easier than I had ever done before in my entire life.

Maybe my body had difficulty adjusting to a slower pace of life? Who knows? Maybe that's why I got sick.

Whatever the reason, for a good solid week I was, indeed, very ill but by the second week I was beginning to feel a little better. The vomiting and diarrhea were tyrants of the past. I no longer felt compelled to stay glued to my bed. For short periods each afternoon, before my daughters arrived, I donned my warm chenille robe and I ventured outside to the backyard where I sat on the garden bench beside the yellow quartz boulder which rested beneath the Lilac Hummingtree. As was my custom, I communed with my Lord.

In the evenings after one or the other daughter had returned to her own home I relaxed in the luxurious, new whirlpool tub. I knew when I bought it that the tub was an extravagance. It was out of character for me to be impulsive but the salesman had been very handsome and agreeable. Flattery does not come often to a woman of my years and experience. There was no doubt he had a silver tongue and I confess he was hard to resist. Besides, when he told me I deserved the luxury of a Jacuzzi I was inclined to agree with him.

Of course it worried my daughters that I was so easily convinced to part with my money. There were many better uses they could think of for my meager savings.

"Your property taxes are due, Mom," Sandi cautioned. "Have you kept enough in your account to cover the taxes?"

"Of course I have, Sandi," I snapped. "Don't you think I know how to manage my money? I've been doing it for longer than you've been alive."

My daughter, Carol, could not stay silent. "You promised Lucien a holiday in the spring, Mom. You haven't forgotten, have you? You don't want to disappoint your only grandchild."

"Of course I've kept enough money aside for Lucien's vacation, Carol. Do you think I've lost my senses?"

She didn't answer my question. Instead she looked at me with a resignation that made me feel like a criminal for spending my money on something I wanted for myself.

The salesman had assured me that I deserved the luxury of a whirlpool tub and I believed him. But the comments of my daughters made me feel, not for the first time, like a selfish, self-centred, old woman who cared for no one but herself.

Soon I put those self-deprecating feelings behind me and I never regretted the money spent on the purchase. I loved the relaxing time I spent in my whirlpool tub. In any event I was in the Jacuzzi just a couple of nights ago when both daughters surprised me with an evening visit.

"It's just us, Mom!" they shouted in unison from the hallway downstairs.

"I'm in the tub," I yelled back.

"We're putting the kettle on. When you've finished your soak come on down for a cup of tea," Carol offered. "Sandi and I have something we want to discuss with you."

Something they want to discuss with me? Oh, oh, that sounds serious.

I pulled the plug, stood up, grabbed my bath towel from the rack and, wrapping it around me, I stepped out onto the softness of the chenille bath mat. Once the bath water finished its gurgling journey down the drain I could overhear the voices of my children. They were speaking quietly but there was something surreptitious about their conversation. I had a funny feeling they were planning some kind of a sneak attack on me.

Immediately I began to think I was becoming paranoid; imagining plots against me by my own children.

Not for the first time in my life, I wondered, *am I losing it?*

"She's not going to like it," I heard Sandi say.

"I think she will be receptive once we explain it all to her," Carol responded.

"I hope so. After all, it's for her own good," Sandi said.

"Of course it is. Of course it is," Carol agreed.

What's for my own good?

I wasted no time drying myself and, wrapped up warm in my chenille robe, I was on my way down the stairs when I heard Carol whisper, "Shhh, she's coming."

Prepared for battle I entered my kitchen to find both young women sitting at the kitchen table. They had made a pot of green tea and I saw some of my favourite date squares set out in an inviting display on one of my glass plates.

"Oh, you brought date squares! Thank you, girls." My enthusiasm was genuine but my suspicions were raised. I was accustomed to them visiting after work in the afternoons. And I had grown used to them taking turns and coming one daughter at a time. The very fact of this surprise evening visit was suspicious. I vowed to keep my mind alert at all times. I knew they wanted something. Just what that was, I didn't know but I had a feeling I was soon to find out.

"Sit down, Mom. Let me pour you a cup of tea." Carol offered.

"How are you feeling now, Mom? Are you over the flu at last?" Sandi enquired.

"Yes, dear, I am feeling much better, thank you. And a cup of tea sounds good too. What brings you girls here tonight? I'm not used to seeing you in the evening."

"There is something we want to discuss with you, Mom."

"Well, this sounds very formal. Should I have dressed for the occasion?" I joked.

They both laughed but not for long. I could see that they were here on very serious business. "So what's up?"

My daughters looked at each other and I knew they were debating who should speak first.

"It's okay," I assured them. "The suspense is killing me. Spill the beans!"

"Okay, since I'm the eldest I'll start." Taking a deep breath, Carol asked, "Have you ever thought of selling this old house, Mom?"

Oh, so that's what they were up to? Well, I'll nip this in the bud.

"No," I answered.

Sandi jumped in with, "Well, maybe it is something that deserves some thought, Mom."

"Why?"

"There is a lot of work and expense involved in keeping this old house in reasonable shape. Neither Carol nor I have enough time to look after the place what with our heavy workloads and all."

"And who asked you to look after my place?"

"We've been here every day for the last two weeks, Mom," Carol spoke up.

"You've been here because I've had the flu for goodness sakes, girls! And it has been very kind of both of you to give of your time. I appreciate that you were both willing to come on over to help me out. But I don't always have the flu and I am perfectly capable of looking after myself and taking care of my own home, thank you very much."

"Don't be angry, Mom," Sandi insisted. "We are just thinking of what is best for you."

"I know very well what is best for me, young lady. And selling my house is not on my agenda. Maybe when I grow too old to look after things I will feel otherwise but right now I am absolutely fine and dandy with the way things are."

"Have you heard about the new retirement home in town, Mom? It's a beautiful place with a swimming pool, gardens to enjoy and lots of people your own age for companionship."

"No, and I'm not interested in hearing about it either."

My daughters shared what I interpreted as guilty looks but it was Sandi who confessed what they had been up to. "We've made an appointment for you, Mom," she said.

[165]

"An appointment? What are you talking about, an appointment? An appointment with whom?"

"With Jason Knobest, Mom. He's the managing director of The Hawkwind Retirement Resort."

"You made the appointment. Now you can cancel the appointment," I told them.

"We can't cancel, Mom," Carol stated.

"It's too late to cancel," Sandi confirmed.

"What are you talking about?" I insisted.

Again they shared what I call that *guilty look.* "He'll be here any minute," they both shouted.

"What?"

"Just hear him out, Mom," Carol begged.

"I think you will like what he has to say," Sandi said.

"I doubt that very much," I replied.

At that moment the doorbell rang. "I'm not answering that door!" I shouted. "I'm not even dressed for goodness sakes."

"You look fine, Mom," Carol assured me.

"I'll get the door," Sandi said and left the kitchen.

I sat, furious, at the kitchen table. I felt ganged up on and powerless in my own home. I didn't want to meet this Mr. Knobest but, suddenly, there he was standing in the doorway demanding my attention and worming his way into my home with his greasy smile and gratuitous greeting.

"Good evening, Mrs. Dawson. May I introduce myself? I am Jason Knobest. I am the Managing Director of The Hawkwind Retirement Resort. What a pleasure to meet you. May I call you Ellen?"

"No, you may not," I snapped.

"Just give him a chance, Mom," Sandi beseeched.

"Please, Mom," Carol pleaded.

I felt trapped. "Okay, Mr. Knobest, say what you have to say but please don't take too long because I am getting tired and will soon want to get to my bed."

"Thank you, Mrs. Dawson. I won't beat about the bush or lead you down a false trail. I'll get right to the point."

"Please do."

"Your daughters invited me here this evening to talk to you about Hawkwind Retirement Resort's wonderful facilities and to invite you to come, on a day and time convenient to you, on a tour of our new premises. Trust me. It's for your own good, Ellen. Your children have your best interest at heart."

"I've already told my daughters that I have no desire to sell my house and move into a retirement home, Mr. Knobest. There is nothing you can say that will convince me to change my mind so I suggest you leave now and not waste anymore of your valuable time or mine."

"From the little acorn a mighty oak grows, Ellen. If you will allow me to plant a tiny seed of information into your mind, I believe you will be surprised by all that Hawkwind has to offer. Will you not give me twenty minutes of your valuable time now or, if you prefer, I can come back at a time that is more convenient to you."

"Mr. Knobest, that is a wonderful suggestion. Please come by twenty years from now. Maybe by then I will be open to hearing all about your hallowed Hawkwind."

He laughed! The nerve of the man!

"Please Ellen, call me Jason. I'm sure your daughters have given a lot of thought to this matter before they set up the appointment for this evening."

I turned my attention away from Jason Knobest and rested my hurt, angry eyes first upon my elder daughter, Carol, and, secondly, upon my youngest girl, Sandi. I said nothing. My unwavering stare said it all just as it had years ago when I'd said, "It's time for bed so put those toys away now." They understood my stare then and they understood now.

I looked into their eyes and wondered why; why are you doing this to me?

And it was as if they heard my thoughts. Carol spoke first.

"We made the appointment last week, Mom, when you were very ill. Sandi and I discussed it. We toured the retirement home. We believed we were doing what was best for you."

Sandi added, "I'm sorry, Mom. We jumped the gun. Will you forgive us?"

"Please forgive us, Mom. We've made a terrible blunder and we apologize."

I said nothing but turned away from my daughters' despair and feeling much more in control of the situation now, I said, "Won't you join us for a cup of tea, Jason?"

"Why, yes, thank you, Ellen," he replied.

"Come girls, come back to the table," I invited. "I know you meant well and, yes, all is forgiven."

"Thank you, Mom," they answered and as the four of us sat around the kitchen table that evening I took a closer look at this Jason Knobest. My daughters are not the only ones who can develop ulterior motives.

"Jason," I asked, "I imagine that as the managing director of The Hawkwind Retirement Resort you make a comfortable living?"

"Oh, yes, Ellen. And, more important, I enjoy the work."

"Are you a married man, Jason?"

"No, not yet, Ellen. My career seems to demand too much of my time."

"Jason, did you know that my daughter, Sandi, is single too? "

"Mom!" Sandi shrieked. "Stop it! What do you think you are doing?"

"Well, Sandi," I answered, "I was thinking of setting up an appointment for you to meet with Jason one evening this week in order for you to get to know each other a little better."

"Mrs. Dawson, I assure you I am capable of making my own dates!" Jason interrupted.

"Mom, what do you think you are doing? My dating life is my personal business. You have no right to set up appointments for me!"

"Oh, is that right, Sandi? And do you agree with Sandi's statement, Carol?"

"Of course I do, Mom."

"And you, Jason? Do you not think a mother has the right to arrange a date for her daughter?"

"Well, Ellen, I believe your daughters are both capable of making their own dates."

"I see, Jason. So all three of you agree that it is wrong for one person to make an appointment for another without the other's consent?"

"Absolutely!" They all concurred.

"I rest my case, children. Now if you will all excuse me, my bed awaits. Be sure you lock the front door when you leave the house. Goodnight."

"Goodnight, Mom, and I am truly sorry," Sandi said with a smile and a hug.

"I know you are, Sandi."

"I love you, Mom, and I'll never do it again," Carol promised.

"I know you won't, Carol."

"Ellen, please accept my humble apology," Mr. Knobest offered.

"Apology accepted, Jason. And you can leave a brochure if you like. I will take a look at it and, who knows, maybe the day will come when a tour of The Hawkwind Retirement Resort will be just what the doctor ordered."

TEN

TEN:

The Hella Chopper:

I was bound and determined to suck her soiled words into the bag as I pushed and prodded the vacuum cleaner from one room in the house to another that hot, summer morning. I poured her anger into the watering can, mixed it with my own, and splashed it onto the houseplants. I carried her hurtful accusation outside and tossed it into the garbage can with the rest of the trash. At the end of the morning I had a clean house but my muddled mind was polluted with hurt, guilt and shame.

Was it all my fault?

By the time noon rolled around I knew school would be out and Lucien would soon be home from his kindergarten class. I was worn out; plain exhausted so I simply threw together some quick peanut butter and jelly sandwiches and poured a glass of milk for my grandson. I had his meal ready for him on the kitchen table when he came through the back door. It didn't take him long to eat and once he had finished his lunch I settled him into his bed for an afternoon nap.

Hot! It was too hot. I roamed throughout the house going from room to room pulling the drapes in order to close out the sun. I closed the horizontal blinds in the living-room at the front of the house and lifted open the windows in the dining-room and kitchen at the back hoping to catch even the slightest breeze if there was such a thing in existence that sweltering afternoon. In June. Soon school would be out for summer vacation. The sun was relentless. It beat like a drum on the roof of my little house. Then I remember another house; one where Jerry never did repair the vent on the roof.

Was that my fault too?

It was too darn hot to do a whole lot more inside the house that day. Once I knew my grandson was sound asleep I secured the front door to ensure his safety. Then through the back door I made my way into the quiet of the backyard. I crossed the brick patio then began my descent down the hot concrete steps all the time keeping my eye on the white wooden bench which was nestled on the green grassy area beneath my Hummingtree.

I was still not fully recovered; still reeling from the unfairness, the harshness of the morning's verbal attack. I needed some quiet alone time to digest the condemning charges my daughter had hurled at me as she shot out the door, slamming it behind her, on the way to work that morning.

"It's all your fault!" Carol had screamed. "Peter would still be with me today if you had just minded your own business. Always meddling! Snooping and sticking your nose into my marriage where it didn't belong! And now, because of you, I'm a single mom.

Lucien is without a father just like I was and it's all your fault!"

"I stood up for you. I took your side, Carol."

Was it my fault because I took sides?

"You never knew when to just butt out and keep yourself to yourself!"

Pain pierced my mind and engraved itself on my soul like the word, *flour*, on a burlap bag. Her scalding attack burnt my heavy heart.

My mind in a daze, I walked as though carried by some unseen force. In this way I carried my hurt and sadness down the concrete steps to the bottom level of the backyard. It was cooler here. The shade from the Maples that filled the bush behind my garden fence offered comforting shelter as I allowed my weary, overweight body to plunk itself down onto the white, wooden, garden bench. The fragrance of the Lilac blossoms overhead was a balm that soothed my shattered nerves.

I stretched out my right arm and allowed my tired, freckled hand to rest upon the yellow quartz rock. In spite of summer's heat my rock was cool to the touch. I could depend on my rock. It was always cool and always calm.

"Are you there, God? It's me again, Ellen."

Just as I had come to expect, the vibration began at the foot of the Hummingtree. He did not let me down. The quivering climbed and made its way up the trunk of the Lilac and in simultaneous fashion the trembling travelled from my feet, up through my legs, and into my body. As the branches, leaves and flowers on the Hummingtree shone translucent, this very healing light shone round about me and I felt one with my tree, my rock and my Lord.

"She blames me. And it's just like you said, Lord. The sins of the fathers are passing from one generation to another in this family. Lord knows with my daddy up in the northern wilderness throughout most of my childhood I learned little of the ways of a man. And when he died I was just a kid. Seems I was still just a kid when I married Jerry. And, Lord, what did I know of Jerry? Is it my fault he left me that stormy night? Was it fate that caused Peter to leave Carol just because Jerry left me? Dear God, how do I break this cycle of misery and shame?"

"Ellen, why do you talk about blame and fault? Have I not said to you, *That ye may be the children of your Father which is in heaven: for He maketh his sun to rise on the evil and on the good, and sendeth rain on the just and on the unjust?*"

"Yes, Lord, I do remember reading that New Testament verse in the Book of Matthew but what does it mean? Carol blames me for her marriage break-up. Is it possible that, because I could not keep my own marriage intact, my children will be cursed to share the

[176]

same fate?   Family patterns are so hard to alter, Lord. Am I asking for the impossible?"

"Ellen, you talk to me about curses and fate. My child, where is your faith? I understand it goes against your human nature, and it takes genuine concern, to pray for blessing and to love your enemy but I know you can do this. Just let it go. Let it go and let me handle this for you."

"I'm trying to let it go, Lord. I want to hand it all over to you but when Carol told me this morning that everything was my fault, I collapsed under her accusation. Dear God, is it my fault that poor little Lucien is growing up without a father's love?"

"Ellen, you must forego these thoughts of fault and blame. My child, pray for fairness and soundness in thinking. Know that Carol loves you just as you love her. Know that you both love Lucien and this is what the child will know. I promise you, Lucien will not grow up without a father's love. Am I not his Heavenly Father?"

"Yes, Lord."

"The temptation to heap blame and fault, especially upon yourself, is strong but know that your faith is stronger."

"Yes, Lord, but what should I do? "

"Let go and let me take care of this for you, Ellen. Love your children and love your grandson. No matter what comes your way, continue to love. I am preparing you for future responsibilities, Ellen, and this is what I want from you."

"Yes, Lord. I'll try. I'll try harder. I promise I will."

"Go in peace, my child."

I felt much lighter after my little talk with God. I got up from my bench and was on my way back into the house when I heard a tremendous, heavy, persistent roar pouring down upon the earth from the heavens. *Oh, my God, what is happening?*

I raced through the house to where I believed my grandson was sleeping. "Lucien! Lucien, wake up child!" I shouted as I ran.

He was no longer asleep. Sitting up on his little bed he was shouting through his fear. "Gram! Hurry Gram! I'm scared."

I raced into the bedroom and lifted the crying Lucien up into my arms. The noise was growing louder, louder and louder. The roar overhead was deafening now.

What on earth?

I set Lucien down on his feet and taking his hand, I ordered, "Run Lucien! Run as fast as you can! Let's get out of the house! We must see what is happening."

[178]

"You're pulling too hard, Gram! Don't pull my arm off!"

"I'm sorry, my boy! But run, Lucien. Run faster than you have ever run before!"

We left the bedroom, tore through the living-room, out the front door and onto the wooden verandah that faced the residential street. The unfamiliar, deafening sound became louder. All up and down the street people came out of their houses. Many were walking about on the road. That's when I noticed that they were pointing up into the sky. They appeared to be in awe. What were they seeing that I couldn't see from this vantage point?

Is it the end of the world?

"Come, Lucien! We must get off the veranda so that we can see what everyone else is seeing in the sky."

"I'm scared, Gram. My ears are hurting."

I lifted him up into my arms and clomped down the verandah steps to join my fearful neighbours on the street. When I looked up into the sky I was wrapped in absolute amazement.

"Look, Gram," Lucien pointed as he shouted. "It's a hella chopper!"

And, indeed, the boy was right. Overhead a helicopter hovered dangerously close to the roofs of the houses. There was nowhere to go, nowhere to hide and there was no way I could think of to protect my grandson from imminent danger.

God, help us! You are my rock! We need you, Lord!

The helicopter thundered overhead. I looked at the terrified, waxy, white faces of my neighbours. And I swear I could hear His words, *that ye may be the children of your Father which is in heaven.*

"Dear God, you said you were preparing me for future responsibilities but I didn't know you were going to scare us all to death!"

I am convinced we are going to die.

The sound became louder and louder. I held Lucien tighter. With his little arms squeezing my neck, I lowered myself to the ground. "Lay down on the road, Lucien."

Such a good little boy, he obeyed my instruction. As I knelt on all fours and stretched my large body above his tiny frame to create a protective barrier I prayed that the boy be spared.

And then the sound stopped.

Silence.

"Oh, my God!" a neighbour cried.

"Run! Run!" another shouted.

There was much clamour and confusion. The silent helicopter began its final descent.

The crash sounded like the ranting of the devil himself. When I dared to open my eyes I could see the rancid smoke as it rose from the flames that licked the leaves of the Maples in the bush behind my house and the homes of my neighbours.

I raised myself up from the ground. Reaching out I helped the terrified Lucien to his feet. "It's okay, my little man. We are saved! It's okay, Lucien."

In what seemed no time at all the fire trucks, police cars and ambulances filled the air with screaming sirens and the street with reassuring, positive action. "Move back, folks! Back from the road!"

Out of chaos came order.

Lucien asked, "Gram, what about the pilot of the hella chopper? Is he okay?"

A policeman overheard Lucien's question and the negative nod of his head gave me the answer.

The miraculous truth of the matter was that with absolute precision the helicopter pilot had ensured the safety of the neighbourhood. He sacrificed himself by crashing into the trees that filled the green space between residential streets.

What do I tell the boy? And then I remembered my conversation beneath the Hummingtree earlier that day. God had said, "No matter what comes your way continue to love."

I looked down at my little grandson. I could not love the boy more than I did in that very moment. "Yes, Lucien, the pilot is okay. He has gone home to live with his Father in Heaven."

I later learned that two people were killed in this crash. I thought about their families and how sad they must be in the knowledge that their husband or wife, brother or sister, son or daughter; their pilot was not coming home.

My first impulse was to find fault and blame someone. Why do so many helicopters crash? Why are young people so quickly taken from their families?

I held Lucien's hand and led him back, up onto the veranda then into the house. "Come through to the kitchen, Lucien, and I will pour you a glass of milk. Would you like a cookie with your milk?

"Yes, Gram."

I placed the milk and a plate containing a couple of Oreos onto the table. Lucien had returned from his room and with him he had brought his drawing pad and colourful crayons,

As I sat at the kitchen table drinking my tea I kept a close watch on Lucien as he sat across from me and drew, with crayons, pictures of the helicopter's crash landing. My eye was on my grandson but my thoughts were sitting on the bench beside the yellow quartz rock in the backyard. Again, but this time with gratitude, I recalled my morning conversation with the Lord.

Once again I heard His question, ""Ellen, why do you talk about blame and fault?" Once more I listened to His instruction, "You must forego these thoughts, my child. Instead pray for fairness and soundness in thinking."

It was while Lucien and I were sitting at the kitchen table that Carol burst into the house and forced me back into the present.

"Mom, oh, Mom, thank God you are okay." Sweeping Lucien into her arms she cried, "My baby, my boy! Were you scared, Lucien?"

"Hi Mom," Lucien smiled. "The hella chopper crashed in the bush right behind our house! It was scary but not so scary 'cause Gram went to sleep on top of me right in the middle of the road so I was safe underneath."

In that moment Carol put my grandson back down on his chair where he continued to colour his drawings. Our eyes locked and she made her way around the table to where I was sitting. Tears flowed like a river from my eyes now as I opened my arms and embraced my little girl.

"I'm sorry about this morning, Mom. I didn't mean the nasty things I said to you. Thank God you are okay. I love you, Mom."

"Don't be sorry, Carol," I responded. "Let's put the morning behind us. What is important now is that we are here. We are alive and we are together. Let it go, love."

At that moment my daughter, Sandi, arrived. "I heard it on the news, Mom. Oh, my God, are you guys okay?"

"God is good, Sandi," I responded. "We are safe and we are together."

"Look, Mom!" Lucien shouted in prideful excitement. "Look what I drew! It's a hella chopper! I drew a hella chopper, Mom!"

"Yes, I can see that, son," Carol replied.

[184]

I looked at Lucien's picture. Then I looked with love at my children and my grandson. I closed my eyes and in silence I whispered, *Thank you, God.* Then I opened my eyes and what did I see? I saw only love. I saw family.

ELEVEN

ELEVEN:

__Lost and Found__:

      My ears are burning. I simply cannot believe the dirty, dastardly and downright nasty things certain people around town are saying about me and Jethro. It seems some folks lead sorry, empty lives and have nothing better to do than to spread cruddy gossip like thick, sticky manure on a hot, summer sidewalk. Outright lies leap from one mouth to another's ear and soon everybody is talking. Do they know what they are talking about? No! But that doesn't seem to make a fiddler's fart of a difference. The tales are told with utter disregard for the truth.

      The blind are leading the blind and God help anyone who tries to get in the way and put a stop to the rumor-mongering. The more often the story is repeated the greater the accusation. Can't they see for themselves that Jethro is an old man, for goodness sakes?

      Do the neighbours forget that Jethro Tunkel is old enough to be my father? There is absolutely nothing more than shared friendship between Jethro and me but, of course, the simple truth wouldn't give the nosy neighbours something to wag their talkative tongues about.

      The only other Jethro I have ever heard of was the Biblical Jethro who was Zipporah's father. If I have

Ellen and The Hummingtree

anything at all in common with Zipporah it's that I'm still waiting to meet my Moses. There is not one ounce of romance between Jethro and me. Sometimes the small town whispering campaign has my mind tumbling in turbidity. I know I should pay no attention whatsoever to what all these idle mouths are whispering but the false rumors and malicious lies have left me livid.

Jethro has been living in my home for almost a year now. I've told you about his arrival and I've told you he came into my life at a time when I was way past my wits' end. Jerry had left me. My daughters were grown and out on their own. Bill collectors were hound dogs sniffing in my empty cupboards. Joy had abandoned me. I wanted to die. If someone had walked through my front door carrying a coffin I would have lifted the lid, climbed in without hesitation and lay down my weary head.

Thanks to Jethro, all that has changed now and the total transformation took place because of this dear man's arrival at my garden gate that summer afternoon. Now that he shares it with me, my life is something worth waking up for in the morning. My life has become something worth living.

Jethro filled two cups from the pot of tea he has made and we are sitting together at the kitchen table enjoying the hot chamomile. Until this day life had become a quiet, pleasant routine for each of us. I'm doing okay financially these days. Although I am managing to make ends meet God knows that, just like

[188]

everybody else, I can always make good use of some extra money. Jethro and I had often day-dreamed and talked about what we would do if we ever had a winning ticket but in my heart of hearts I never ever expected to really win a lottery.

Of course, I'm happy and excited about winning the big lottery. That afternoon when I told him I held the winning ticket Jethro jumped up out of his chair. He was the Cheshire cat doing his happy dance right there in the middle of the kitchen floor. I believe he is more excited than I am and that is saying something.

It's a very big prize and I believe it is possibly big enough to be life-changing. As happy as I am, at the same time I am feeling concerned and upset. What has me feeling less than good is the fact that in order to collect my big prize I will have to leave my small town and travel by bus all the way to Toronto. The good Lord knows I am afraid of big cities; afraid of muggings and even afraid of crossing busy city streets.

Jethro is convinced a cup of hot tea will calm me down. He gave his happy dance a rest and said, "Come now, my girl, let's both sit back down at the table. Drink your tea."

"I don't want to go to Toronto, Jethro, but it seems that's the only way I can collect my winnings."

"Don't worry, Ellen. It's a long time since I've been in the big smoke but I will be there right beside you. I'll take care of things and you will have no worries. I'll ride the bus with you to the city to cash in your ticket," he says with a squint that is intended to be a wink accompanied by a mischievous smile that does its best to peek its way through his snowy white beard. His good-natured squint lifted my sinking spirits.

"I need to meditate on this, Jethro. I haven't been outside of this town for more than twenty years. I'm scared to find out who I am inside city sophistication. I'm afraid I'll get lost in all the commotion of people rushing here, there and everywhere. I might disappear in the crowd and never find myself again. And, Jethro, Lord knows how all that money will change my life. There is nothing wrong with the way things are and I'm not so sure I want it changed."

Jethro is a clever man with an amazing gift for memorization. He loves to store obscure quotations in his creative, intelligent mind. He may be short in stature but I'm aware he is never short in finding the right words to make me see my world in a more positive light. His next question makes a liar out of my awareness.

"Ever hear of Oswald Chambers?" he asks.

I look up into Jethro's deep brown eyes and say, "The only Oswald I've ever heard of is Lee Harvey; the one that Killed President Kennedy. And that's another reason I don't want to travel to Toronto; big cities are filled with murderers!"

Even at five foot four Jethro is taller than me. I haven't taken the time to measure my height in a long time. I know I used to be five foot two but I think I started shrinking at an earlier age than most women. Now Jethro stands there looking down upon my ignorance.

"No, no, Oswald Chambers was born way back in 1874. He had a gift for making magic with language and he had a special way of putting words together."

"I don't need to be reminded that I'm getting old, Jethro, but that's a little before my time. Besides, what has Oswald Chambers got to do with me making a trip into big city crime and squalor?"

"Just listen to this, Ellen."

"You going to give me another one of your famous quotations, Jethro?"

"Yep, I might be an old man but my memory is not a sack of wet noodles yet. Now listen to this. Chambers says, *We say, let me get back to the duck pond, to its limitations, where all is so simple and placid and easy to understand. We may go back to our duck pond and be a success there, but God wants to launch us out into the ocean.*"

My blank stare should say it all but I utter the words anyway. "I know it's a big win but I've got no plans to go wasting money on any ocean cruise, Jethro."

Of course he laughs.

"Don't you see, Ellen? This small town is the duck pond and you haven't been exactly thrilled with all the nasty talk that's been going on around here lately. It would do you good to get away for a few days. Try out your wings in the *ocean of commotion* in Toronto."

"I don't know, Jethro. I've got a lot to do around here."

"Ellen, you are just making excuses. *'The whole point of getting things done is knowing what to leave undone.'*"

"Always a quotation! Jethro, please leave me be for a while. I'm going out into the backyard. I need some time alone. It's obvious to me, if not to you, that I'm not ready to make such a big decision."

I leave Jethro sitting alone at the kitchen table. I open the back door; make my way across the deck and down the concrete steps to the bottom of the yard. My bare footsteps across the soft green grass send the chipmunk scooting into the garden wall. I see Raven watching me from the treetop in the woods behind my backyard fence. I'm wearing my favourite green sundress and the heat of the summer sun massages my tired, aching shoulders.

I've made a big win! Hit the jackpot! I should be overjoyed. I know I should be feeling happy and carefree. Instead I feel like I am carrying all the worries of the world on my back.

I step out of the sunshine and into the solace of shade beneath the lovely Lilac. The fragrance of the purple blossoms invites me to sit on the bench beneath my Hummingtree. I sit and stare at the beauty of the Spirea, the Forsythia and the crawling purple Thyme that hugs the ground along the retaining wall's edge. I ask myself, *why would anyone in her right mind want to leave the peace and beauty of this garden to visit city clutter, crime, clack and clatter?*

Not for all the money in the world would I want to live there. But am I willing to visit Toronto, the modern day Sodom and Gomorrah, for all the money in the world?

I reach out and touch the cool calm of my yellow quartz boulder.

"Hi God, I need a few minutes of your time. It's me again, Ellen."

God's response is as fast as my faith. At once I am wrapped in the healing hum and vibration which soon fills my mind, body and spirit. I pray for His help and within moments my fear is over-ruled and replaced with the assurance of His love and guidance no matter where in the world I may roam. I listened to his soft yet strong words. *Be still and know that I am God.*

"Yes, my Lord. I am trying to be still but I am fearful about a trip to Toronto. What should I do, Lord?"

Look into your heart, dear child, and look into your own hand. Don't you know the answer is in your hand?

In my hand? I raise my arms and stare at the stretched-out fingers on my freckled, sunburned hands. I turn my hands over and stare at the pink palms. "My hands are empty, Lord."

Empty your heart of worry, Ellen. Only then will it be filled with the love you are truly seeking.

The love I am truly seeking? I was unaware that I was looking for love but I received and wrapped those words around me.

There are many people you could help along the way with that money, Ellen. You could ensure your grandson's education and help your daughters to have an easier time of it.

Of course God's wisdom made me realize that my fear was something I needed to overcome. I needed to replace it with my love for the family. "Thank you, Lord," I said.

It was a beautiful warm afternoon. For more than twenty minutes I stayed sitting on my garden bench beside the huge, yellow quartz rock beneath the fragrance of the Lilac tree. Once it was made I journeyed back into the house to share my decision with Jethro.

Back in the kitchen, I find him still sitting with his elbows resting on the old kitchen table, hands occupied with the caressing of his shaggy beard.

"Can you be ready to leave in the morning?" I ask. "I'm going to call the bus station now and get an up-to-date schedule. We, my friend, are going to travel to Toronto."

Without saying a word Jethro gets up from the old, wooden kitchen chair and retrieves his old beat-up guitar from the corner of the room beside the old humming refrigerator. I hear him singing, *"I'm pickin' up good vibrations. She's giving me excitations."* While I dial the bus station's number he is singing The Beach Boys' *Good Vibrations*.

"Sshhh! Be quiet Jethro! It's one of those darn answering machines and I've got to be able to hear which button to push!"

The following morning we are ready to go. We are about to climb into the taxi that will take us to the bus station when, like Lot's wife, I can't resist the urge to look back. And when I do, I feel frozen, like I've turned into a pillar of salt. I see my nosy neighbour, Emma, staring through the slats of her venetians. I swear she has more eyes than a pineapple. Jethro and me leaving town together for a few days just adds fuel to the infuriating fire. This journey is going to give lots of fresh fodder to the small-minded old cows who think I'm living in Sodom and Gomorrah no matter where in the world I am or how chaste I remain.

The journey from home is a long one. We need to change buses three times but once we are finally settled in the third bus I give a satisfied sigh of relief. Jethro and I are both pleased when the driver tells us we will be given a couple of food and bathroom stops along the way.

At the bus station I held tight to my beige, leather purse. When we boarded the large Greyhound bus I was able to choose a comfortable window seat midway down the aisle. Jethro is right behind me and he sits empty-handed beside me in the aisle seat.

"Got your ticket?" he asks.

"I gave my ticket to the driver," I answer.

"Not your bus ticket," he whispers. "The big one."

I pat my purse and give Jethro a knowing nod. Then darned if he doesn't start singing again. *"If money talks, it aint on speaking terms with me."*

Surprised, I ask, "Are you jealous of my big win, Jethro?"

"Hey, don't you know me any better than that by now?"

"Of course I do," I said.

[196]

And I did.

A few days earlier I had watched the movie matinee, City of Joy, on T.V. Now as I sit in the bus staring out the window at the passing countryside I think about Hasari's bus trip to Calcutta and I remember the words of his father telling him, *"If the journey is not what you expected, do not be surprised."*

I understand the necessity of Hasari's decision to travel into the unknown. Sitting beside Jethro now I feel the fear of Hasari's wife. At the same time I feel the excitement of his children. I'm day-dreaming as I remember in the movie what turned out to be a prophetic question. *What if this journey is not what I expect?*

Do I have expectations? Do I really want the windfall that has led me to be sitting on this bus? While I continue to look through the window and watch as country begins to turn into city I realize once again that all this money will be life-changing. Do I really want my life to change?

Soon all trace of country living is smothered beneath high-rise monuments to man's greed and governance.

Jethro reaches over and taps me on the knee. "We're here."

I look out the bus window and see the constant movement of the multitudes. I allow all the hustling, bustling bus passengers to leave the bus before I feel

[197]

ready to leave my seat. Jethro, standing in the aisle, is a grey-bearded Cheshire cat. "We're here," he repeats as he extends his arm encouraging me to get up out of the safety of my seat.

It is time for me to prepare to leave the bus. With one hand I pat my hair into place while with the other I take his proffered hand. We walk through the crowded city bus terminal. Jethro holds the door open for me and soon I am outside. I am standing on Bay Street in downtown Toronto. I tilt my head back to look up into the dizzy heights at the monster buildings stretching up into smoggy grey clouds.

I'm feeling light-headed. When Jethro reaches out to steady me as I wobble on uncertain legs he says, "You're just a little dizzy because you're hungry, that's all. Let's start this adventure by finding ourselves a restaurant and having a good meal. I don't mind telling you I'm hungry as a horse."

"Good idea, Jethro," I say. "I could eat a little light lunch."

With no specific destination in mind we begin walking northward along Bay Street.

"A big, heavy one for me, Ellen. Breakfast was a long time ago," Jethro says.

Immediately I think of the high price of food in Toronto restaurants. Lifting my hand to pat my purse is an automatic but also a worthless gesture. Not only have I left the sunshine back at home I have also left my beige, leather purse on the bus.

I can't believe my own carelessness and stupidity. I stood still and cried, "Jethro, I've left my purse on the bus."

Well, have you ever seen a short, bearded, bow-legged old man and an overweight, middle-aged high-heeled woman unaccustomed to being anything but barefoot race hand in hand through city streets?

No, and you would not have this day either. Jethro and I do not even attempt to run.

Overwhelmed by disappointment, I creep to the city sidewalk's curb and allow my bent body to slump to the cracked concrete. Feet in Bay Street's gutter I sit on the sidewalk, hold my head in my hands, and I weep. Not knowing what else to do, Jethro sits down on the sidewalk beside me.

"Hope no car runs over our toes," he says.

It was all I needed to hear. I'm sure Emma and all her fickle friends back home could hear me laughing.

Jethro's soft voice was soothing to my soul as he began to sing lyrics from the old Beatles song, *"Cause I don't care too much for money. Money can't buy me love."*

He stood up on the sidewalk and in a princely manner he extended his arm offering me his hand. "Allow me to buy you lunch, Ellen."

I look at my hands and from somewhere far away I remember the words, *the answer is in your hands.* On this day I can't remember the answer. Indeed I have no clear memory of the question but deep down in my heart I know the importance of hand-holding. He extended his arm and offered me his hand.

I know I always feel safe when holding Jethro's hand. I know that once I take his hand I will feel at home. I will know I am in good hands.

Jethro holds my hand. I am a child again but this time I know I will not be abandoned.

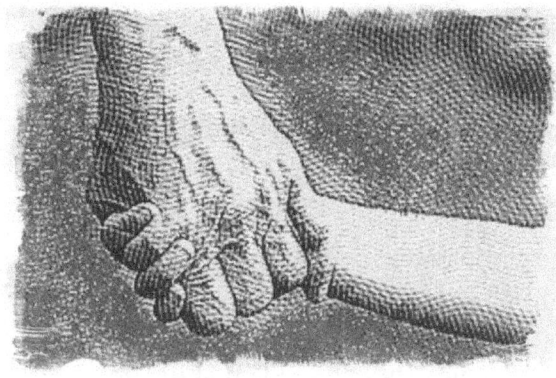

I remember the prophetic statement, *"If the journey is not what you expected, do not be surprised."*

But I am surprised. I stand on busy Bay Street and look into Jethro's eyes. I do not hear the traffic swishing past. I don't see the people scurrying in all directions. I lose myself in Jethro's eyes and I see nothing but love. In that instant I realize that even though I have lost the big winning ticket I am recipient of a gift that is priceless.

Jethro continued to hold my hand.

My first thought is, *Oh, my! Did Emma and those gossipy old girls see something that I have not allowed myself to see? Will I now validate their unwelcome assumptions?*

I would like to tell you that upon our return to the bus station someone had possessed the honesty and the decency to turn into the authorities my beige, leather purse which contained the winning ticket but that is not what happened. Fact is I never did find my purse. I never did collect on my big win.

I would like to tell you that upon our return to our small town Jethro and I began to share a mad passionate love affair which turned the scandalous tittle-tattle nattering into awesome authenticity but that is not what happened either.

What did happen is that the day I lost my purse, I found abiding love.

The neighbours still natter but I am not interested in listening to their prattle. I sometimes wish that everything they gossip about would contain even a tiny iota of truth but of how much sinning do they think an overweight middle-aged woman and an old man are capable? Yes, Jethro and I have our moments but the moments are swift and the interludes long; nothing at all even close to what the gossips believed we got up to.

But there is one very important thing we did get up to and that is our adoption of the beautiful Black German Shepherd, Kris. But this was many years later when I, like Jethro, was also beginning to grow old. I was seventy-one and my dear Jethro many years my senior the day Kris first made his home with us. I give you my word I will tell you much more about Kris later.

But for now as I wash the lunch dishes, under my breath I sing *"A victim of my time, a product of my age,"* Santana's lyrics of the song, *Nothing At All* while

[202]

Jethro strums his guitar and sings, *"Love is a many splendored thing."*

It is obvious to me that he and I hold a different perspective on life and on our relationship but we are both content. It was a happy day for me when I realized that the answer truly was in my hands. I learned that lesson on the day that Jethro held my hand in his own.

While Jethro sings his songs and memorizes his quotations, I love to sit on the bench beneath my Hummingtree. I don't listen to the rumor mongers. Instead I listen to the still voice within. I sit quietly on my garden bench and talk to God. I thank Him for His love and for the love I continue to see resting in Jethro's deep brown eyes. I may not be wealthy but, indeed, I am rich.

TWELVE

TWELVE:

Vault of the Heavens:

Marielle was my cousin but to say she is my sister, to tell you she is my best friend, or to claim her as my soul mate does not begin to describe the bond we shared. I loved her with all my heart. We were very close. When Marielle died it was as though a thieving marauder slashed open my chest and chipped a huge chunk out of my heart; that piece which enabled me to feel empathy, identification and, indeed, even understanding of a human's will to carry on.

I don't remember the day I first met her because, after all, I was a newborn babe. She was four years old the day my dear mother, Eva MacPherson, gave life to such a one as me.

Marielle wasted no time in making her decision to dislike me on that very day when I first felt the sun's rays on my infant face. She later told me why. It was because my crimson, crying eyes demanded everyone's attention. No one, not even her own mother, was offering Marielle the slightest consideration. All eyes focused on me, the new child. The green-eyed monster filled her heart and as the seasons changed from summer to autumn, to winter and at last to the springs of many childhood years her love for me, if indeed it ever existed, remained covert.

Yet I adored her. I wanted to be with her. To her everlasting embarrassment and frustration, I wanted to follow her everywhere she went.

Throughout most of my turbulent, searching, growing up years she continued to resent my very existence. When I was much older she admitted to me that she had not wanted to be bothered with what she termed an emotionally needy child like me.

"You were always such a cry-baby," she stated, hands on hips, in her own inimitable, don't argue with me, do as you're told, matter of fact manner.

Her confession brought us closer together but I had no need to be told that for all those years I was unwanted. This was something I always knew. As a little girl I felt abandonment deep down in a stomach that ached for her attention. I would have welcomed anyone's attention but it was Marielle I loved and it was Marielle's attention I craved.

I wanted her to love me in return. I wanted her to hold my hand and walk home from school with me but instead she would say, "Get lost, Ellen! Go play in traffic!"

One day when I was six years old she was ordered by her mother to take me along with her and her friends to the local swimming pool. Marielle did not want me to come with her and although this happened more than fifty years ago I have clear remembrance that her friends were not overjoyed to have me there with them either.

"You always gotta drag her along with us!" one friend complained.

"Why don't you get lost, kid?" another shouted.

I wanted Marielle to tell her friends to shut up. I wanted her to tell me she loved being with me but, of course, that did not happen. No one cared what I wanted, least of all, Marielle. What she said to her friends was, "Yeah, I always get stuck with her. She's nothin' but a pain in the neck!"

I remember we arrived at the swimming pool that day. It seemed to me we had walked a very long way along Toronto's busy, steamy sidewalks to get there. As soon as I saw the gigantic pool for the first time I immediately wanted to go home. The enormous swimming pool was filled with noisy, pushy children; kids a lot bigger than me. And that water looked way too deep. I was scared.

"I want to go home, Marielle."

"Well, you're not going home! We just got here so don't be stupid. Just be quiet." she insisted.

"I want to go home!" I was crying again.

"Ellen, for pete's sake, we just got here! Stop your bawling."

I looked at the deep, blue water in the huge, cavernous, cement swimming pool. It might just as well have been a witch's cauldron. I was scared to death. "I want to go home!" I sobbed.

"Well, I'm not taking you home."

I stopped crying, wiped my face with the back of my hand and became defiant. "I'll go myself then!"

"You will not!"

"I will!"

I could see that my stubbornness scared her. She was hesitant. "Marielle, come on in! The water's fantastic!" her friends were shouting.

"Are you sure you know the way home?" she asked me.

At last she was relenting. "I do," I swore.

"When you leave the pool just walk straight along the sidewalk until you come to the first street with a stoplight and there you turn right and keep walking until you come to our street. Okay?"

"Okay," I smiled.

"Remember now! Turn right at the very first stoplight."

"I will," I promised.

I was going home. I walked and I walked. Then I travelled further. I journeyed until I felt very tired. That's when I started to cry. I had forgotten to turn right and by now I had crossed at many green lights. I was very lost. Tears stuck to my face like Velcro.

But God smiled down on me from His welkin and sent a kind stranger to pick me up off the city sidewalk. My rescue could have been a tragedy but thank God this stranger was a good, caring family man. He carried me into a variety store where the owner made me a big strawberry ice cream cone and allowed me to sit atop the cooler. And that's exactly where I was when my mother arrived to take me home.

Marielle was punished by her father for allowing me to leave the swimming pool alone. It was many years before she at last forgave me for creating so much trouble and chaos in her life that day.

I valued her gift of forgiveness. I had waited for a very long time and this gift did not arrive until we were no longer children. Accepting her love and forgiveness we then, as young adults, began to become better acquainted. It wasn't long at all before we became the very best of friends. We discovered that we had a lot in common and it was a joy to find out that we shared many common bonds.

Years passed and the time came when we each married and had children. Throughout this time though we didn't see each other as often as I would have liked, we did spend hours talking on the telephone together.

And as we both began to grow older we shared our deepest dreams, thoughts and aspirations. Marielle was an avid church-goer. She never wanted to miss a Sunday service. I wasn't so keen on attending church however in spite of this, Marielle and I discovered that we were, in fact, kindred spirits who traveled a very similar spiritual path.

Marielle is the only one who did not laugh at me when I told her about my conversations with God through the yellow quartz rock beneath the Hummingtree. She was intrigued and wanted to share in my experience. I invited her to share the backyard bench with me on several occasions. She found it a peaceful interlude but said, "I don't feel any vibration and I don't hear any humming."

I knew Marielle wanted to experience these things and by sharing this knowledge she made me appreciate the awareness that my Hummingtree was there for me alone.

What Marielle did possess and enjoy was a gift for the art of cooking and it was through the sharing of her culinary gifts that I became a passable cook. She taught me how to make the most delicious meat pies and one year our pies won first prize in a food competition at our annual church bazaar. We remained best friends throughout our adult lives.

Life sped by. I was approaching retirement age the day Marielle told me she had lung cancer. I did not want to believe her. My ears ached. They were on fire. "I don't want to hear this," I cried.

For many long, painful months my Marielle held onto the breath of life. She talked to me of her absolute knowing that there is new life when this old one is finished. We sat together in the garden and looked up in awe at God's star studded vault of the heavens.

Marielle died.

Anger consumed me. I sat on my bench beside the rock beneath the purple Lilac.

"Why God?" I cried. "Why did you take Marielle away from me?"

I reached out angry arms and touched the yellow quartz rock. Within seconds I felt the vibrations. They began at my feet and worked their way up until my body was swallowed. I trembled. Soon I am the vibration.

"I want her with me, God," I begged.

"Ellen, Ellen, Ellen," God answered. "You need to accept. It is my will that must be done on Earth.

Then I remembered my Lord's prayer, *"Thy will be done on earth as it is in heaven..."*

"But why, God? Why did you have to take my Marielle?"

"There is a reason for everything, Ellen. I thought this was a lesson you had already learned. Do you so easily forget?"

"I want her with me," I cried in vain.

The spirit whispered in my ear, *"Be still and know that I am God."*

"God, if you cannot, if you will not, give Marielle back to me then please, Lord, take me too. I want to be with her." Silence swallowed me. Frustration filled me. "God, are you listening to me?"

"I hear your prayer, Ellen. But it is not your time to leave this planet. You still have lots of work to do here."

"I want to go with her, Lord."

And then the old memory of the long trek to the swimming pool knocked on the door of my mind and made itself at home. It was such a huge memory that there was no room inside my thoughts for anything else to reside.

"You wanted to go with her that long ago day too, Ellen," the Lord reminded.

"I know I did and I still do want to go with her, God."

"You wanted to go with her and when you arrived at the swimming pool you wanted to go home again."

"I was a child then. I'm older now and I'm wiser. I want to go with her, Lord."

"Not yet, Ellen. Not yet."

Hearing Spirit tell me *not yet* brought back memory of the day when Marielle had told me about her initial experience with meditation. "I sat on the floor and wound up my legs in a yoga-like fashion and I talked to God, "she said. "I told the Lord, '*I want to learn patience and I want to learn it right now.*' But God said no. He said, no, Marielle, not yet. Ellen, I didn't learn a darn thing. After five minutes I gave up."

I sat there on my garden bench and laughed aloud. This memory of her telling sustained my laughter.

"It is good to hear you laugh, my child. You need to laugh more often," the good Lord said.

"Will I go to be with Marielle soon?" I dared to ask.

"You will go when I say it is time for you to go," he answered.

For a very long time that day I sat in subdued silence on my bench in the garden beneath the Hummingtree.   Soon I felt warmed by God's presence. I felt lost in the silence. Acceptance began creeping and crawling into my heart. Acceptance was beginning to heal the jagged edges left by the raider who had chip, chipped away until the knife had cut deep into my heart centre.

And then Spirit spoke again. "It will rain when I say it rains and the sun will shine when I say it shines. When I declare clouds vanish, the clouds shall be moved and the sun shall rule the heavens. Learn this lesson well, dear Ellen. I repeat! You will go when I say it is time for you to go!"

"Yes, Lord, I hear you. But I miss her. I miss my Marielle."

"She is not far from you, my child. Close your eyes and you will see her. Close your ears and you will hear her laughter. Close your mouth and you will hear her speak. She is not far from you, my child."

And so I continued to sit on my garden bench for a very long time. I closed my eyes, my ears and my mouth. I opened my mind, my heart and my soul. And there she was.

And there she is whenever I need her. I talk to her and I say, "I want to go with you, Marielle."

She replies, "Always tagging after me, you are! Not yet, Ellen. Not yet. You will be called when it is your time to return to your heavenly home. It is not up to me and it is not for you to decide when. It is only God who holds the key to the vault of the heavens."

THIRTEEN

THIRTEEN:

Just a Sliver

Yes, indeed, memories dance and wake up my tired old mind whenever I think of my dear cousin, Marielle. There is one memory in particular that stands out and I want to share it with you. This memory still gives me a giggle today. I will share remembrance of this day when we had both left middle-age behind and made ourselves at home in the unpredictable realm of the senior citizen. On this memorable day Marielle, in her wisdom, decided to spike the meat pies.

"It's a sure-fire, enduring recipe for calamity, Marielle!" I insisted.

"Hush, Ellen! Nobody's going to know the devil's darn difference!" Pointing her authoritative finger she ordered, "Now drag that pine stool over here. I want you to climb up onto it and get me old George's bottle of Seagram's Five Star Rye Whiskey. You can't miss it. It's at the back of the top shelf in behind the pickling jars."

Feet planted in righteous stubbornness I insisted, "No, Marielle! I've read the recipe and it calls for beef, mushrooms and red wine; not Rye whiskey! Nobody puts whiskey into meat pies. It's unheard of!"

"Do you want to travel all the way into town again to buy some red wine, Ellen?

"I wouldn't be caught dead in a liquor store."

"That's just what I thought you would say!"

"Why not just substitute with some apple or grape juice?"

"Because I want to win this contest, that's why! Now stop wasting time! Climb up onto that stool, Ellen, and get that Rye whiskey down for me."

With a heavy sigh I crossed the spotless, worn linoleum covered kitchen floor to the stool that sat silent in the corner beside the broom closet. Knees creaked when I stooped over to grab hold of the scratchy seat of the pine stool. I thought about that long-ago day when Marielle's boarder, George, had brought the brand new stool into Marielle's house. I also thought about lifting it but the osteoporosis in my low back decided I had better not entertain that thought for long. Instead I took my time dragging it behind me toward Marielle whose impatient, flour-covered hands were just about ready to slap me silly.

"I haven't got all day, Ellen!"

I shuffled my old, pink, fur-trimmed leather slippers a little slower along the kitchen's linoleum and mumbled, "Supposed to add the wine while you're cooking the beef stew; not after the pie filling is cooked."

"Makes no difference," Marielle insisted.

[218]

"Does too, Marielle! Supposed to cook the alcohol away and just leave the flavor of the wine."

"Never mind that! Anyway it's too late now and I told you nobody will know the difference. I've already cooked the beef stew. I just finished thickening it with flour and now it's ready to pour into the pie shells you baked this morning. We've got enough mixture here for four pies; three for the fair and one for us," she said as she turned on the kitchen tap to wash the flour off her busy hands.

"If you insist on using George's old whiskey in the pies then I don't want anyone to know I had any part in their making. Don't you dare tell anyone! You're the one that will need to be held accountable; not me! Leave me out of it!"

"Don't be any more foolish than you have to be, Ellen, and hurry up with that stool."

I lined the stool up against the yellow painted kitchen cupboards. The top of the stool was about five inches lower than the well-worn arborite counter top. Toes pointing north and south, I planted my feet on the floor, opened the cupboard door and, wishing I was much taller than the five feet, two inches God gave me, I cricked my neck to stare up at the top shelf. "I'm not climbing up on this old stool," I decided aloud.

Marielle was just a few years older than me. Being the elder made her word gospel as far as she was concerned. "Come on, Ellen, climb on up. I'll hold your legs. I won't let you fall."

"You want the whiskey? Then you do the climbing, Marielle!"

I knew she didn't like to think about her weight but Marielle was a good fifty pounds heavier than me. "You're lighter, Ellen. Lighter and younger! Why do you have to be so cantankerous and hard to get along with? Come on now, girl!"

"Oh, all right!" I relented as I leaned my upper body over the kitchen counter. Raising my right leg I managed to get my right knee up onto the stool's top surface. I brought my left leg up and locked it in place beside the right. Both knees on the stool I raised my right arm into the air and cried, "Can't even reach the second shelf; never mind the top one."

Marielle stood behind the resistant me and with both hands began pushing and prodding my rear end in an effort to hoist me into an upward motion. "You have to stand up, Ellen!"

"Stand up? I may be nuts but I know I'm not that crazy. I am not going to stand up on this stool, Marielle! And stop pushing my bum!"

Just then Marielle had a brainstorm. "See if you can get yourself up onto the kitchen counter, Ellen. The stool and the counter make like a ladder. Climb, Ellen, climb up. You just need to get yourself up one step higher."

"Dumb fool idea!" I retorted. "Should have brought the ladder in from the yard!" With trepidation I raised my right knee up from the safety of the stool's top surface. While Marielle nudged and shoved, I somehow managed to get myself hefted up on all fours atop the kitchen counter. I could only imagine what I looked like. I know I felt like a fool. "Now what?"

Marielle could not contain her laughter. "Just stay put while I go grab my camera."

"Don't you dare!"

"Okay, okay. But, Ellen, you can't reach anything poised like a cow in pasture. You've got to stand up. I won't let you fall; I promise. I'll hold your legs steady. Stand up on the counter."

I raised myself up onto my knees. Reaching up with my right hand I could just barely touch the bottom tip of the cupboard's top shelf.

"Come on, Ellen, I'm holding you. I won't let you fall. I promise you won't fall."

Legs shaking, I managed to lift my right leg and place my right foot flat atop the kitchen counter. Now I felt like a nervous groom down on one knee ready to propose marriage. Reaching up I could now touch the top shelf but in the process of raising my right arm my head automatically caused my eyes to stare downward at the arborite counter top. "Can't see a darn thing!"

"Ellen, you just have to stand up on the counter. I won't let you fall. I'll hold your legs."

"Marielle, no! I'm not moving another inch! You get yourself out into the yard and bring that ladder into the kitchen. Should have done that in the first place!"

"Oh, all right. But that ladder is a heavy one. I just hope I can lift it by myself."

Marielle left the kitchen.

I later learned that once out in the backyard she spotted the ladder on its side leaning against the shed. She told me one end of the rusty old extension ladder was lodged in behind the unlidded metal garbage can. She knew she needed to move the can before she could retrieve the ladder. Ordinarily that would be an easy

[222]

feat but it had rained overnight and the garbage can contained at least five or ten gallons of rainwater. She couldn't budge it.

Finally she leaned her heavy body against the shed, extended one leg and pushed against the can with her foot. She pushed and shoved until at long last the garbage can overturned. Water soaked the earth around her feet but that was of no consequence to Marielle. Now she was able to get a good hold on the old extension ladder. It was longer than she remembered it being; and much heavier. It was not an easy task but somehow she succeeded in carrying the ladder through the back door and into the kitchen.

"Good grief, Marielle!" I shouted as she entered. "You need to shorten that ladder. It's too long. No way will it stand up in this kitchen."

She scratched her head and asked, "How on earth do I do that?"

Frozen on hands and knees atop the kitchen counter I shouted out directions. "There's a rope running up the centre of the ladder, Marielle. Do you see it?"

"Yes, I see it."

Check the knot. Is it frayed?"

"No, it's okay, I think."

"Okay, now there are locks on either side of the ladder. You need to unlock them and push the ends of the ladder together to make it shorter."

"Locks are all rusted! This is going to take me all day, Ellen. Please won't you just stand up on the counter top? I promise I'll hold your legs and I won't let you fall. Please Ellen."

"Oh, all right. It's always me giving in to you, Marielle. Been that way all my life and I'm sick to death of it!"

Marielle left the ladder where it was on the kitchen floor and returned to where I was plunked on all fours atop the counter. She took a firm hold on my body and pushed. "Okay, now one foot at a time. Raise yourself up to a squat."

I squatted.

"Should have just used grape juice!" I yelled as I attempted to stand on shaky legs.

With her shoulder under my bum Marielle pushed. When she thought I was high enough she used both hands to push me further upward until at last I succeeded in standing up straight atop the counter. The top of my head was just an inch or two from the tiled drop ceiling.

"Now what?"

"Seagrams Five Star Rye Whiskey is at the back of the top shelf. I remember it was more than half full when I took it away from old George after he passed out that long ago night."

"He wasn't passed out, Marielle. He was dead."

"How was I supposed to know that, Ellen? I never should have taken in a boarder anyway and I told you so at the time. Now pass me down the pickling bottles one at a time until you can reach the whiskey bottle."

"You were always hard on George. Wouldn't have hurt you to show a little kindness toward him," I answered but I did as I was told. Soon the old kitchen table was half-covered with pickling jars. "I see it now," I shouted.

"Good! Now pass me down that whiskey."

I passed the bottle to my determined cousin. It was more than three-quarters full. Couldn't have been George's only bottle that night, I thought, as I waited for Marielle to pass the pickling jars back up to me. Top shelf in order once more, I fearfully lowered myself back down, first onto my knees, then onto all fours. With Marielle's guidance I stretched out one leg until my right foot landed atop the stool.

"Should have been a circus performer!" I cried when at last I felt both feet grounded on the kitchen linoleum.

[225]

Scrubbing her hands with Sunlight soap under the kitchen tap Marielle removed all traces of the rusty extension ladder, my shoes and the dusty pickling jars. Her eye on the prize, she then uncapped the whiskey bottle. "How much do you think I should put into the beef stew, Ellen?"

"I still think you should use juice, Marielle. The stew is already cooked. This alcohol is not going to burn off!"

"Makes no never mind! Not a whit of difference! I'm just not sure how much I should use and, Ellen, you are not a lot of help in this decision-making. It's a big pot of stew and not a lot of whiskey."

Then without further hesitation she emptied the bottle of its contents into the large pot of beef stew. She took her wooden spoon and gave it a good stirring before ladling the mixture into my pre-baked pie shells. She then laid the strips of cooked pastry creating pretty patterns across the top of the stew. She repeated this process and soon the four meat pies rested on the kitchen table. "First prize, Ellen! We're going to get it this year for sure!"

Visualizing intoxicated judges passing out ribbons, I wondered if we would ever be able to hold our heads high and set foot inside our church again. "We're going to get it all right," I said, "but it may not be the prize you've got in mind, Marielle."

"We're only allowed three submissions. This pie is for our supper tonight," Marielle announced setting one pie aside. "Help me get the rest of them out to the car, Ellen."

Once back inside the kitchen we sat on padded chrome chairs at the table. "This is a day we will always remember, Ellen."

"No doubt," I responded with a grimace.

"Maybe we should taste this pie before we take the others to the fairground. What do you think?"

"Not me, Marielle. You know very well I'm teetotal."

"Mixed in with all the other flavours you won't even taste the whiskey, Ellen. Come on, what do you say?" Marielle got up from the table and retrieved the pie knife from the kitchen drawer.

While Marielle sliced the pie, I allowed myself to reminisce and think of dear old George. It was more than ten years since he had journeyed to his greater reward and I missed him more than I would ever let on to my cousin. She thinks she does but she doesn't know it all. Why, she doesn't even know the half of it. She only thinks she knows everything. To Marielle, George was just a paying boarder; an old drunk but a fellow whose financial contribution helped to pay off her mortgage on this old house.

My cousin knew me well but she was unaware that I nurtured other warmer, loving memories. I remembered the tender touch of George's hand on my arm; the soft, mellow sound of his singing while he strummed his guitar and serenaded me on hot summer nights. Most of all I remembered the inviting soft, warm wetness of his lips on mine. All these memories were created long ago and long after Marielle lay snoring in her bed.

"Come on, just a little piece," Marielle insisted. "Hey, what's the matter with you, Ellen? A little whiskey won't kill you. It's nothing to cry about."

I hadn't realized that I was crying. The uninvited tears slipped past my cheeks in silent surrender. I could feel his warmth and see George's smile as I said, "Okay, but just a sliver."

That evening after Marielle was sound asleep I made my way to my bench beneath the Hummingtree.

"Are you there, God? It's me again."

I heard the vibration making its way up the tree simultaneous with the vibration moving throughout my body. My ear to the yellow quartz rock I heard God say, "I'm listening, my child."

"Dear God," I cried, "I miss George. I think I even loved him despite his many faults. And, God, I'm sorry about eating a sliver of the spiked meat pie tonight. I have no excuse. Do you forgive me?"

"Ellen," He replied in His soft, reassuring whisper, "if you could see me now what do you think you would see?"

"A scowl, my Lord?"

"No, dear Ellen. You would see me smile. You need more days like this one in your life, my child. Life is to be lived. Life is to be enjoyed."

I returned to my own home the following day and prepared to go with Marielle to the church bazaar. As you know, I was never what you would call a churchy person. Marielle never used to be either when she was young but in her later years she never missed a Sunday. She picked me up on her way to the church hall. Before that day I had never witnessed such jovial judging. Yes, the judges loved our meat pies and no one was happier than my dear cousin, Marielle, when, just as she predicted, our meat pies took first place in the final judging.

Later that evening I sat alone in my backyard on the bench beneath the Lilac Hummingtree. As I thought about the events leading up to our acceptance of that red ribbon I couldn't help but giggle. Then, when I least expected it, through my yellow quartz rock I heard my Lord say, "It's good to hear you laugh again, Ellen."

FOURTEEN

FOURTEEN:

Foray into Technical Territory

Jethro Tunkel was my partner and he was also my very best friend. He was out walking our newly acquired pet dog one day just a few months ago as was his custom ever since Kris moved into our home and our hearts. Kris was a lovable, gentle boy. Jethro and I were thankful that he was also obedient.

We almost did not accept Kris into our home as a family member; certainly not because of any fault attributable to the five year old black German Shepherd but simply because of our age. I was seventy-two the afternoon we invited Kris home and, of course, Jethro was several years my senior. Our hesitation in adopting this fine lad was fear-based. For us it was a frightening prospect because we were afraid we would not out-live this lively pet. We were fearful that we might leave God's good earth before Kris did, thereby leaving him homeless. We knew he deserved better than that.

But our hearts melted when we made Kris's acquaintance. A shake-a-paw and a few loving licks on our faces were all we needed to make a prompt decision. No discussion was required. We had made our decision. It was love at first sight.

Since Kris was already five years old and we were told that most of his breed lived to be hopefully ten to twelve years of age, Jethro and I decided that we would make every effort to keep up with this active fellow and surely, we thought, we would find the energy to do so for at least another seven years.

As was his custom Jethro was taking Kris for his morning walk one day last month. I wasn't present to observe what happened but a friendly neighbour later reported to me that she saw everything.

"One minute Jethro and Kris were on their way down the well-trodden path. You know the spot where many prior years of footsteps had carved steps into the gently sloping hillside toward the woods. One minute they were on their way down and the next minute Jethro collapsed. I could see him. He was lying face down on the ground," she said.

I was told that Kris didn't move. He stayed right there with him, licking his master's face in an effort to wake him up in order to continue their walk.

Jethro did not wake up.

Again I was left alone; no, not alone this time because the beautiful Kris remains steadfast, loyal and loving. But I miss my Jethro. Yes, Kris is a faithful companion but, to me, the house devoid of Jethro's laughter, quotations and songs, feels as empty as a politician's promise.

After Jethro's death my daughters, Sandi and Carol, would come to visit but their lives were busy. Their visits were few and far between and usually kept short. "We are not staying long," they would announce before they were even half-way through the front door.

It was my grandson, Lucien, who surprised me on one of his visits with a gift; one that was about to change my world. By now Lucien was a very successful businessman. He was expert in many fields about which I knew absolutely nothing. One of these areas of expertise was the fast-paced world of the computer.

He arrived that morning, grinning from ear to ear, with the cardboard covered parcel in his hands. "I've brought you a present, Gram!"

"Oh my, Lucien! You shouldn't be spending your hard-earned money on me!"

[233]

"Trust me, Gram, this is money well spent. I give you my word; you are going to love it."

He carried the well-wrapped package to my kitchen table and began the process of opening it. I hovered around him like a hummingbird, eager to see what was in store for me. Kris hovered beside me and together we kept all eyes on the table as layers of brown paper and myriad tiny styrofoam snowballs littered its top as well as the linoleum floor beneath.

Then it was all unwrapped. The gift was revealed. It was open on the table in plain view. Lucien looked to me for appreciation and approval.

"What do you think, Gram?"

"I don't know what to think, Lucien. You know how much I appreciate your thoughtfulness and generosity but what on earth is that thing?"

His booming laughter filled the room. Kris wagged his tail; a reflection of Lucien's pleasure. "It's a laptop, Gram."

"Hmm. A laptop? "

Yes, I had seen TV commercials about laptops but I hadn't paid too much attention to them. I believe my blank stare told my Lucien all he needed to know.

"Don't worry, Gram. I will teach you. It's not as complicated as you might think. Mom tells me you have been writing some stories and now, with the computer laptop, you will be able to say good-bye to that ancient Remington typewriter."

"But Lucien, I like my typewriter."

"I know you like your typewriter but you are going to love this laptop! You will even be able to interleave in order to include illustrations for your stories."

"Interleave? Lucien, what on earth does that mean?"

"Don't worry, Gram. I'll teach you everything you need to know. You will be a professional in no time."

Yes, that is how it all started. Receiving Lucien's gift was my first step in the process. True to his word Lucien got me hooked up with an Internet service. He installed what he called software though I've no idea why it was so named or what was soft about it. It wasn't as though I could feel it. Lucien told me this software had a name. It was called Microsoft Word and it was on this software that he taught me how to re-type all my hard copy stories so that I would have them all in one file on my laptop. I have to admit I was very impressed and in this regard I remain quite satisfied as I remember that life-changing day.

Lucien set me up with an email account and he visited often enough to teach me some of the basics of navigating the infamous Internet. This old dog not only learned a lot of new tricks but I also became reasonably proficient in learning a new language. I learned how to surf the net; how to like and share on Facebook; and how to chat with friends I had never before met in my life.

I never knew there were so many abbreviations but I was learning that in order to be proficient in this new on-line lingo I needed to know how to shorten almost everything I wanted to say. I learned that it was NP to say OMG, I'll BRB. I learned how to make smileys and pretty little hearts and when someone in the chat room made a humorous comment I was able to ROFL along with the best of them.

Lucien was proud of me and he encouraged me when he observed the way I was able to catch on quickly to this new way of communicating; not that I ever allowed this new obsession to interfere with my times of meditation upon my garden bench beside the rock beneath my beautiful Lilac. But I do confess I often lost track of time while exploring the Internet with my new laptop. This was a different kind of timelessness; one, I realized, that could very easily become addictive.

Yes, he encouraged me but he also warned me of danger. He talked about viruses and told me that under no circumstances was I to open attachments from people I did not know.

"Well, Lucien," I said, "How will I get to know people if I am afraid to open their emails?"

"Just be careful, Gram," he cautioned. "Especially in that chat room you've started to visit. Don't give out too much personal information and, for heavens' sakes, Gram, don't send any money to anyone."

Lucien's generous gift of the laptop, arriving when it did, helped me very much to carry on my life without Jethro's love and companionship. I felt proud of myself that at the age of seventy-two years I was becoming a much more prolific writer. I began to create a website and I learned the basics of blogging. And I wrote my many short stories while Kris patiently sat beside me awaiting his play time in the backyard.

Kris missed Jethro who had always taken him for his daily walks. I did my best to fill Jethro's shoes in Kris's life but I soon learned that even twenty minutes of brisk walking was well over my limit. I know Kris missed the longer walks Jethro had shared with him. When we returned home I would sit on my bench beneath the Lilac to meditate. I carried my new Internet lingo into my communion with God. "OMG, maybe I am too old to be what Kris needs in his life."

The good Lord listened to my old woman groanings and then He taught me that He is not only a loving God but He also has a great sense of humour. "NP, Ellen," he responded. "If you can navigate around the Internet you can challenge yourself to navigate the trail through the woods with Kris. He's good for you. He gets you up off that chair and into nature where you need to be."

I did strive to create a balance in my life and in that of Kris. I wrote my stories, surfed the net and I became not only proficient but also social in the chat room. And each day I put aside the time to throw the ball and walk the trails and play in the backyard with Kris. Everything was going very well in my life together with Kris until that day when Gregory's email arrived.

I first met Gregory Hamilton in a senior's chat room. By this time I had learned to navigate the site and I had read Gregory's profile which informed me that he was seventy-three years old, a widower with grown children and grandchildren. He lived far from my small Canadian town in the small village of Windle in the Borough of St. Helens in Lancashire County, England.

He was a pleasant fellow and I enjoyed chatting with him. With so many miles between us our developing friendship certainly seemed harmless enough to me. He told me a lot about his little village. "Population of just over three thousand souls, Ellen," he said, or should I say he typed.

I shared with him about my family and I told him a little about my small Ontario town. We were both surprised to learn that in the past our towns had once been much more prosperous than they were today. They had both been mining towns. In my case the miners sought uranium while in Windle they mined for coal. "We call them Burgies, Ellen," he said.

"And just what is a Burgie, Gregory?"

"Burgies are tailings on the site of the old Rushy Park Coal Mine site.

"Were you a miner then?

"No, I was never a miner," Gregory informed me. "I'm long retired now but I used to work for a glass manufacturing company. These tailings I've told you about were caused by the dumping of the toxic chemical waste created from the manufacture of glass. But of course today it is all being well taken care of and you would never guess any damage had been done. The earth is covered in woodland and tall grass today but it was a much different story when I was a young man working in close contact with that toxic waste."

"Is Windle a pretty place?" I asked.

"Today it is that, Ellen. Maybe one day you will come here and see for yourself?"

Amazing that a woman can feel flirty at the age of seventy-two! I am learning that on the Internet anything is possible. "Is that an invitation, Gregory?"

"You would always be made welcome, Ellen."

At that point I thought OMG but I typed BRB.

"Kris, come!" I ordered and with him by my side we left the laptop and ventured out into the backyard. I needed some quiet time to consider Gregory's invitation. A trip to England? Me? A woman who had been afraid to leave my small town to travel with Jethro to Toronto? What insanity is this?

The following day while sitting at my desk and typing my story I decided to rest a bit and check my email. My daughters, Sandi and Carol, now stayed in touch by email as did my grandson, Lucien. Of course none of my family knew what I was up to with Gregory in the chat room. Even I wasn't sure exactly what I was up to but I had to confess that I was enjoying it, whatever it was.

I was surprised that day to see that in addition to messages from my family there was also an email from Gregory. This was the first time he had communicated with me outside of the chat room so I was pleasantly intrigued.

My pleasure turned to sadness when I read his message. "Sorry, Ellen," he wrote. "I'm not feeling well today so I am unable to meet with you in the chat room."

Of course I wrote back to him. In my email I assured him that I understood and I hoped that he would soon be feeling much better.

The following day I received another email from Gregory, this message even more disconcerting than the one before it. "Not well at all, Ellen. On my way to hospital. Do not be too concerned if you don't hear from me for a while."

Naturally I was very concerned and very upset. Although I had never met Gregory in what I had learned to call the *real world* I had grown quite fond of him. It was only because of Kris's companionship and the shared chat room time with Gregory Hamilton that I was able to better deal with the terrible loss of my loving Jethro.

I wrote back to him letting him know that I was keeping him in my thoughts and prayers. I went to the Blue Mountain website and I learned how to send an E-card. I sent a very pretty get well card and to show how much I cared about him I wrote a little poem. The words were simple but from the heart. *Gregory, you are a light in my life; my love for you I'm confessing. I'm sorry to know that you are ill and I send you healing blessings.*

Before I had a chance to even think about retracting my words I clicked on *send.* The deed was done. Then I thought of my mother who had often said, "There's no fool like an old fool!"

I thought of my daughters and somehow knew they would not approve of what I was beginning to think of as on-line love. And then I thought of Lucien and, with this thought, I smiled. I knew he would approve of such a trendy grandmother. I could almost hear him saying, "Rock on, Gram."

After sending this card, several days passed and I received no response from Gregory. Knowing he was in hospital I spent my time walking with Kris. When we were not walking I sat on my garden bench and prayed for Gregory's recovery.

When the third email arrived I was quite surprised as well as concerned to discover that the person typing the email was not Gregory though he was using Gregory's email address to communicate with me. He introduced himself as Walter Goodscam. Yes, I know I should have been tipped off by his odd surname but I'd watched enough old British movies to know that English family names are often very odd and unusual.

Walter wrote, "I'm sorry to inform you that Gregory is extremely ill in hospital. He requires a very expensive surgery; one that on his small pension he cannot begin to afford. He asks that you please help him as much as possible. Please send a bank draft or a money order immediately. Your help in this matter is desperately needed."

Walter had included a mailing address to which I should send my money. For a brief moment I remembered Lucien's warning, "For heavens' sakes, Gram, don't send any money to anyone."

Of course, I brushed his cautionary advice aside. It simply did not apply in this circumstance. Gregory was my friend. And now he was a friend in need.

I didn't have a lot of money living on a fixed income as I did. But by now I owned my home and I lived frugally. That very afternoon I ventured into town where I visited my bank. I purchased a money order for five hundred dollars. I deposited the money order into an envelope and sent it by courier to the address Gregory's friend, Walter, had given me.

Given the expensive hospital bills that would be incurred by Gregory, I knew that five hundred dollars would be a drop in the bucket, but it was the best I could do and, to me, it was a considerable amount of money.

Oddly enough, after I sent this money off to Walter, I never did hear from Gregory again. I began to wonder if he had passed away. I missed him very much and each day when I visited the chat room I would hope to see a message from him. But weeks passed and I heard neither from him nor any news about him.

It was much later in that same year when Kris's barking took me to the front door which I opened to see two uniformed policemen on my doorstep. "Are you Mrs. Dawson?" one enquired.

"I am."

"May we step in and have a word with you?" the other asked.

"About what?"

"About a Mr. Gregory Hamilton, ma'am."

Oh, my, I thought. They are here to inform me that Gregory is dead. "Come in," I said. I directed them both into my living-room. Kris was on his best behaviour. He sat quietly beside one of the officers but I knew he was there to protect me because his eyes stayed focused on both men.

One officer did most of the talking. "You knew a fellow by the name of Gregory Hamilton?" he asked.

"I did."

"And, ma'am, are you familiar with a Mr. Walter Goodscam?"

"Oh, yes," I replied. "Mr. Goodscam is a friend of Mr. Hamilton's."

"I guess you could say that, ma'am," the officer stated. "You see, Mr. Hamilton and Mr. Goodscam are actually one and the same person."

I was left speechless but I guess the officers were able to read the expression on my face.

"You sent money to England, ma'am?"

Feeling like an idiot I could only nod.

"Sorry to tell you that you were duped, Mrs. Dawson; you and many other senior women who visited that chat room."

"Officer, this is so very difficult to believe. Mr. Hamilton was such a lovely, sensitive gentleman. When he became ill I was very concerned about him. I felt it was the least I could do to send him the money his friend requested."

"And how much did you send, ma'am?"

"Five hundred dollars," I responded.

"Mrs. Dawson, your friend Mr. Hamilton, alias Mr. Goodscam, is a twenty-nine year old hoodlum living in Liverpool, England. He has scammed hundreds of senior women like you, all around the world; women he met in chat rooms. Before the authorities caught up with him he had made a fortune. He lived high, drove fast cars and dated faster young women. He was the kind of guy who spent the money more quickly than he kept it coming in. I'm sorry to inform you that there is small probability you will ever see your five hundred dollars again."

So began my first foray into technical territory and so it ended. I wanted to keep the news of my foolishness to myself but, as my luck would have it, reporters got wind of the story and the names of all the duped women, including my own, were published in the papers and splashed across TV screens throughout the world.

Many women were scammed for thousands of dollars. My meager five hundred was a drop in Gregory Hamilton's bucket but it had been a lot of money to me. But the greater theft was the loss of self-confidence I experienced. I had thought I was smarter than that. I had believed I was too old and too wise to be taken in by a scam artist.

As old as I was then, today I am older again and I hope I am a little wiser. I am, at least, wise enough now to stay out of the chat rooms.

I have learned that chat rooms are addictive and they can be a lot of fun. Even though I know better I sometimes feel the urge to go on-line, sign in and chat away. When this urge seems too much to resist I simply say, "Come on, Kris, let's go for a walk."

Tail wagging, always agreeable, Kris accepts my invitation. We walk together in the real world and today my life, though sometimes lonely, is good.

When I feel the need to chat I talk to Kris and when I feel the need to pray I sit on my bench beside my yellow quartz rock beneath the beautiful Lilac and I commune with God who is always there for me.

FIFTEEN

FIFTEEN:

***The Nugget*:**

I was forty-eight years old when my grandson, Lucien, was born to my elder daughter, Carol. It was a joyous time of celebration. But two short October days later my mother, Eva Campbell-MacPherson, died. And how do I feel as I force myself to ingest these near simultaneous mysteries of birth and death? I don't. I can't. Feelings are frozen.

While joy is tossed in one direction, grief in another, I stand alone in the middle, completely devoid of all human emotion. I'm a dichotomy; split like a log at the mercy of the lumberjack's saw.

My life at this time is a train wreck. My husband, Jerry, is long gone. My daughters, Carol and Sandi, are busy living their lives. They don't need me anymore. No one needs me. I'm an unemployed empty-nester wondering how soon the mortgage lender's lock will leave me standing on the wrong side of the door. Abundance has not yet arrived nor do I believe it ever will make its presence known in my life.

God is lost. I have looked and I have searched some more but I can't find Him anywhere. After the funeral I sit alone on my backyard bench beneath the Lilac tree. I reach out to the yellow quartz rock and wait for my Hummingtree to send God's healing warm vibrations throughout my frozen body. I'm clothed in

[248]

hard numbness. Even the power of God's love cannot penetrate my skin of steel.

When I could not find God in my yellow quartz rock I decided I would make an appointment to visit Reverend Wilson. Only on rare occasions did my cousin, Marielle, convince me to attend church services along with her on a Sunday morning. It had been years since I visited his Methodist Church. My faith had long ago floundered in the pews and, until now, it was only through my yellow quartz rock beneath the Hummingtree that I found, felt and heard God's assuring presence.

But this day my rock was silent. Therefore I sat on an overstuffed chair in the minister's cluttered office and looked at Jesus hanging on the wall. Reverend Wilson, bless his soul, did his best to advise me; to point me in the right direction. He sat behind his desk, opened his Bible and quoted from the Old Testament. His soft voice was calm as he read.

"Ellen," he said, "these words are from the Book of Job, chapter, one, and verse 21. *"The Lord gave and now he has taken away. May his name be praised!"*

"Reverend Wilson, you want me to praise God? How do I praise someone I can't even find? He's lost, I tell you!"

"Ellen, please hear me. God is not lost."

Again he reached for his Bible and chose a passage, this time from the New Testament.

"Listen to this, Ellen. *These things I have spoken so that in me you will find peace. The world will make you suffer, but be brave. I have defeated the world.*"

"Those words are from the Book of John, chapter sixteen, and verse thirty-three. Don't you see, Ellen? This is your assurance that God is in control. He is not lost."

Until that day I had forgotten that quoting Bible verses was one of Reverend Wilson's favourite pastimes. It was only then that I remembered he rarely voiced anything resembling original thought in his sermons; always quoting from the Bible and reading from the works of others.

Then I remembered that was one of the reasons I stopped attending his Sunday morning worship services. His words built walls in my mind and they never climbed a wall to touch my heart. Unfortunately, today was no exception.

No, I never found God inside the church. God was always alive and well in my backyard beneath the Hummingtree. I could always commune with Him through my yellow quartz rock. Always; that is until now.

I was in a quandary. Reverend Wilson was no help; no help at all. I was disappointed, not for the first

[250]

time, but I thanked him for his sincere effort to be of some comfort to me. I knew he had done his best and I couldn't blame him for my poor reception. I returned home.

As I once again, with heavy heart, sank my body onto the backyard bench beneath the Lilac I thought about the words Reverend Wilson had shared with me. *God is not lost*, he had repeated to my unhearing ears.

I know I should not have been so insistent. I don't condone my unbending declaration that God is lost. Somewhere very deep within me I did know it was me who was lost. I reached out my arm, placed my hand on the yellow quartz rock and in my pain I cried out, "Help me God! It's me, Ellen. I am so lost!"

There was still no vibration but I felt something within me shift. I lifted my head and closely observed my surroundings. I observed my backyard and found it beautiful. The Lilac's bare branches were a reflection of the empty spaces in my mind and in my heart. Today this umbrella did little to soothe and lift my tiredness. I saw that the yellow forsythia was a clever chipmunk's haven. He thought he was hidden beneath the large branches but I could see his tiny, bright eyes peering out over the garden wall. He was an adorable critter and, on this particular day, his actions taught me the lesson I needed to learn.

At once my old ticker quickened its rhythmic beat. Chipmunk had, indeed, given me an answer. He believed he was hidden from my view. And just like the chipmunk, I believed I was well hidden beneath my sorrow and grief but God saw me searching even when I could not see Him.

"Thank you, Chipmunk," I whispered. For the first time since my mother's death I felt just a little of the happiness the birth of my grandson, Lucien, was offering to me.

I find it hard to believe what I did next. Who or what motivated me? Was it Reverend Wilson's Biblical quotations? Was it the chipmunk's wisdom? Was it God Himself who pushed me up the backyard steps to the back door of my house; carried me through the rooms to my bedroom where I searched through the night table drawer for my mother's old Bible? Maybe it was a combination of all these things.

I now realize everything happens for a reason. Reverend Wilson, the chipmunk, and God Himself were all working together. Everything is one.

Bible in hand I felt as though I were floating through the air as I made my way through the backyard and once again back to my bench beneath the Lilac. I made myself comfortable and then, just as I had done when I was a very little girl, I closed my eyes, opened the Bible and pointed my finger onto the random page.

When I opened my eyes I saw that the Bible was opened to Proverbs. My finger was on Chapter eight, verse three. I read the words, *"She crieth at the gates, at the entry of the city, at the coming in at the doors."*

"She crieth at the gates," I read once again, aloud this time. And at last I was able to cry. I allowed myself to release the pent-up emotions that had been blocking my vision, my rationale and my connection to the good Lord. I reached out my arm once again and placed it onto the warmth of my yellow quartz rock. I heard the vibration as it began in the roots of the Lilac and made its way up the trunk to the beautiful, bareness of its autumnal branches. As I listened I could feel the healing warmth. From the earth it made its way into my feet, up my legs and into my body. The healing power of God reached my heart which melted. Tears dripped from my eyes onto God's good earth.

Then from within me I felt God's presence and reassurance. "The gates, Ellen." He said, "A nugget of wisdom awaits you at the gates. Leave now and go to the gates."

"Gates? What gates, Lord?"

"Read the verse again, Ellen, and you will know what to do."

"Yes, God. Thank you," I whispered in return.

The humming ceased. The vibrations returned to the rock.

Again I read the verse from Proverbs. *"She crieth at the gates, at the entry of the city, at the coming in at the doors."*

I had no understanding but, as God had promised, I knew what to do. Filled with faith I left my backyard and walked down the street. I journeyed through the residential streets of town. I kept walking until I had traversed the busy commercial downtown core. I did not stop walking until I reached the big billboard which sat at the side of the highway on the edge of town. This large signpost is the closest thing we have to a city gate.

The occasional car whizzed past me on the highway but I felt quite unnoticed as I leaned against the post and allowed my body to slide down against it until I was resting upon the green grassy shoulder of the road.

"A nugget of wisdom awaits you at the gate," God had said.

I sat for a very long time. Soon the day's light was making its journey into evening and still I waited. Soon I was wondering why I was waiting. I had heard God's message and I was doing my best to follow His footsteps in faith. Something was wrong. But what? Again I thought of the Bible quotation, *"She crieth at the gates."*

I'm not crying. Is that the problem? Am I supposed to be crying? Is it through my tears that I will discover the nugget of wisdom?

From somewhere in the past I heard someone saying, "Ego, ego, ego!"

Oh, Lord, I thought I could do without a remembrance of my life with Jerry. But the memory persisted.

"It's not always about you!" Jerry had shouted.

Not about me? If not about me, then who?

With more struggle than I liked to admit I raised my overweight body up from the now cool grass. I had been sitting by the billboard's post for hours; waiting, neither knowing what I was waiting for nor when this unknown something would arrive.

When driving along this highway one can see little behind the billboard. I crept in behind it and took a greater look at the unfamiliar landscape. In the distance behind the few trees that stood in line I could see the outline of a figure of someone. *This is very strange,* I think as my feet followed my decision to investigate further.

As I drew closer I could see that the figure kneeling on the dirt was a very old grey-haired native woman. Behind her eyeglasses there were tears. Yes, she was crying. And then my eyes do see remnants of what once must have been a gate. *"She crieth at the gates."*

For hours I, the foolish one, had been waiting at the wrong gate. Now I realized that these gates were at the entrance to an old abandoned cemetery. I had heard about this place but in all my years of living in this town I had never visited here before. Why would anyone want to visit an abandoned burial ground?

Why is this woman here? And why is she crying?

I approached her and when I was just a few feet away from where she was kneeling I stopped in wonder and amazement. I could scarcely believe what I was seeing. I didn't know whether to remain where I was or whether to move closer in order to speak with the elderly lady. It was a difficult thing to know what to do next.

I decided to stay where I was in order to respect the woman's prayerful privacy. Pines, Maples and White Birches mingled together around the clearing that constituted the old burial ground. I could see some gravestones though most were overgrown with God's colourful blanket of weeds and wildflowers.

The crying woman was kneeling beside a rectangular shaped grey stone. The chiseled words were made illegible by years of weather.

I inched myself closer. Now I could see that her brown skinned face was as chiseled as the headstone.

[256]

Looking at her I could not help but think, "This woman is a very old soul. She has met life head on and survived."

I did not mean to; I did not want to; but I could not hold back the invasive cough that began way down in my stomach and worked its way up through my body and out of my mouth.

She turned her head at once and looked at me.

I don't know why but that's when I started to cry again. Perhaps it was the sight of the tearful eyes that met my own. "Hello," is all she said.

"Hello," I replied.

"I'm glad you have come," she said. "I'm growing tired and it is getting chilly. Creator told me someone is coming to receive the gift and I have been waiting a very long time. I'm glad you are here." She smiled.

"My name is Ellen," I told her. "I'm sorry I kept you waiting. I've also been waiting a long time but it's only now I realized that I was waiting at the wrong gate. I wasn't even aware that the gates of this old cemetery existed here."

"It matters not, child. You are here now and that is all we need to know."

"Do you have something for me then?" I dared to ask.

"I do," she replied. "Come sit here with me and hear my story."

I did as she asked. Together we sat on God's good earth while Old Mother told her tale.

"Long ago," she began, "when I was very young, I lived way up north with my people. It was there I met her. She was an old lady from the Cree tribe, named *"Eyes of Fire"*. She taught the *Warriors of the Rainbow* how to live life in the *Way of the Great Spirit.*

At that time, as strange as it seemed to me, there was also a white man who listened to *Eyes of Fire*. I would always remember that his name was Leon MacPherson. He was a trapper who, in his journey, learned of the Great Spirit. He was welcomed and became one with the Warriors of the Rainbow.

As I have said, this was many years ago when I was not much more than a child, you understand. At that time the trapper gave me this gift of a gold nugget. He told me this gift would be mine throughout my life but that before my journey leads me away from this earth I would pass this nugget on to a white woman. He told me this white woman was his daughter and that her name at her time of sacred birth was Ellen Angela MacPherson."

My ears burned with the truth and beauty of her words yet I said nothing as she continued with the mystical tale.

"When I awakened this morning, I sat on the white plastic chair in my yard and Creator came to me and said, *"Your time is near. Today you will give the gift of the nugget to the trapper's daughter."*

I listened to Great Spirit who told me to come to this abandoned sacred place. I did as I was instructed and here I am in this place. I have been here for several hours waiting for you to come.

And now you have arrived and it is time for me to keep my promise made many years ago to the white trapper. Soon it will be the hour when I will meet my maker. I am honoured to pass this along to you. Here is your gift," she said in a very soft voice as she held out her hand.

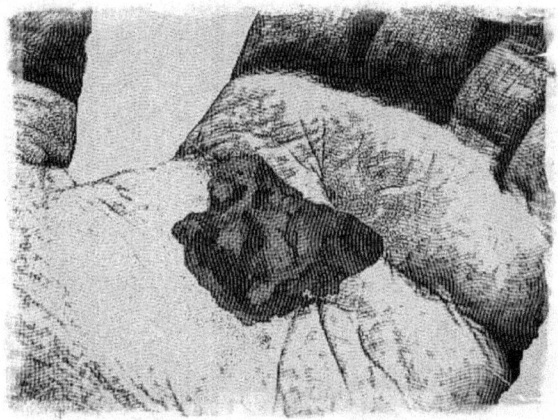

Upon her outstretched hand lay a beautiful gold nugget.

I moved closer to the woman; close enough to extend my arm and wrap my fingers around the nugget. I held the gold piece firmly in my grasp. It was then that I felt as though my father's love was flowing through me. I cried.

"There is a message that accompanies the gold nugget," she said.

I nodded and said, "Yes, I have been told." I stood before the old woman and awaited the nugget of wisdom that I knew would be mine as God had promised.

"The message is this," she continued, "*A mother knows Lucien needs you to live.*"

There I stood by the gates of the abandoned cemetery. I held the golden gift from my father, Leon. I received the wise advice from my mother, Eva, who assured me my new grandson, Lucien, will need me. Through the new babe I would be needed and useful once again.

"God surely does work in mysterious ways, "I said to the native gift-giver."

"Lucien is just name same as Luke. You know this?" she asked.

"Maybe I do," I responded. "Lucien's father is French."

"Luke, you find in the Bible."

"Yes."

"You have a Bible?"

"No, not here. At home I have my mother's Bible."

"Creator tells me to tell you that you must read Luke. Great Spirit gives me a few words from Luke to share with you."

"Please tell me what they are?"

"This I will do. Creator said the words go like this. *"Now you are letting Your servant depart in peace according to Your word for my eyes have seen your salvation, which You have prepared before the face of all peoples."*

"Thank you," I said. "To me, this day is nothing short of a miracle."

Homeward bound I thought; Lucien is born and my dear mother passes away. How do I feel as I allow myself to ingest these near simultaneous mysteries of birth and death? God knows that at last I can feel feelings once more and in my heart of hearts I am grateful. I know I am blessed.

SIXTEEN

SIXTEEN:

I Need You to Remember Me

"You think I don't hear the gossip!" I exclaim in indignation. "What are you trying to insinuate? Just because I'm a little forgetful doesn't mean anything."

"I'm not insinuating anything, Mom. Sandi and I were just talking about an ad we saw in the local paper this morning."

"Ad, schmad! I see the way you two look at each other. Guess I know what's going on! I didn't just fall off the turnip truck!"

"You've got it all wrong, Mom," Sandi intercepts. "When we saw the Hawkwind Retirement Home advertisement Carol and I just thought this would be a good day to take a drive and have a look at the place. It's a long time ago that Jason Knobest came to visit you. In fact it was years ago. Do you remember his visit, Mom?"

"Yes, I remember and do you remember I told you it was not polite to make appointments for other people?"

"We've made no appointment, Mom. We just thought it would be a good day for a drive and we thought it might be pleasant for all of us to have a look at the place. We can drop in there, have a cup of tea and get a bite to eat for lunch before we tour the facilities. Did you know the retirement residence overlooks the inlet? It offers a beautiful view; in fact, I think I will take my camera along. And, Mom, the grassy grounds with the brick walk-ways are ideal for a leisurely stroll by the lake."

"It will do us all some good to get out of the city and enjoy some fresh air," Carol agrees.

"Lots of good places along the lakeshore for a walk if that's what you're looking for," I say. "I know what you're up to! You want to be rid of me! You want to put me into a home!" I can feel my hope for freedom falling. It lands like sediment in the pit at the bottom of my stomach which churns and pushes the declaration up and out through my mouth. "I have a stomach ache! Can't go anywhere today!"

I pull the blue chenille robe's belt tighter until it feels snug around my waist and, leaving the kitchen, I walk through the living-room on the way to my bedroom. Behind me I hear my daughter shout, "It's time to get dressed, Mom. We'll take a nice drive in the car today."

"Have a nice time, dear. Enjoy your drive," I shout back just before closing my bedroom door.

My stomach doesn't feel quite so queasy or heavy once I'm back in my own room. I sit on the bed and, arms by my side; I run my hands back and forth across the silky softness of the bedspread. It's a beautiful, colourful, floral spread. I know it was a gift from somebody. Now who was that? It wasn't all that long ago. Oh, well, no one can be expected to remember everything. Anyway it's not important who it came from. It's not as though I'm planning to give it back.

I get up from my bed and walk over to my dressing table. Opening the middle drawer I rummage for my underwear. It's time to get dressed. I feel like going for a walk. I see my shoes on the floor over by the armchair; the brown, sturdy, comfortable ones. I'll wear them today. Now what am I looking for? I keep rummaging around in the drawer but I can't find it, whatever it is.

Now what was I going to do? Oh, that's right; I will go for a walk. I cross my room, sit in the armchair and ease my feet into the sensible soft-soled shoes.

I leave my bedroom and cross the living-room to the front door. Outside the apartment, in the building's hallway I have to stop and think for a minute. Should I go left or right for the elevator? Silly old fool, I chide myself. I'd forget my own head if it wasn't attached to my neck. Of course the elevator is to my right.

I start walking along the hall when I hear some woman calling me.

"Mom, what are you doing?"

Nosy neighbor! Where does she get off calling me Mom? I'm going to tell Carol about this one. I decide to ignore her. I'm just about at the elevator when the woman grabs my arm.

"Hey, lady," I shout. "Let go of my arm! What's the big idea?"

"Mom, what are you doing?"

"Look lady, I don't know what your problem is but I'm not your mother. Let go of my arm."

"You're not dressed, Mom. You can't go out in your robe!" the woman insists.

I lower my eyes and see that I'm still wearing my blue chenille robe. For heaven's sakes, I put my walking shoes on but I forgot to get dressed.

"I'm going home to get dressed now. I was just on my way," I tell the lady.

"Let me help you, dear," she says.

"I'm not helpless, you know!" But I decide to let her take my arm and guide me back to my apartment. I'm not really sure if I should turn left or right. I've never been very good with directions. I live in apartment 634."

"Yes, I know. I'll take you home, Mom" she says.

"My dear woman, I am not your mother! If you must know, my name is Ellen. And just because I'm old enough to be your mother doesn't give you the right to call me Mom. Only Carol can call me that. Well, Sandi too; but not you!"

The lady starts to weep. "What is your problem?" I ask but she just continues to cry.

I walk down the hall with this crazy, crying woman. We stop at my apartment door and I'm surprised she opens the door of my home and, bold as brass, walks right in; doesn't even knock on the door. The nerve of some people's kids!

My daughter, Sandi, is there in the living-room. I don't get it. She doesn't even seem surprised by the arrival of this strange, unwelome intruder. She says nothing to her or about her. In fact, all she says is, "You need to get dressed, Mom."

"I know that, Sandi."

"We don't like you wandering off on your own like that."

"I wasn't wandering, Sandi. I was going for a walk. Where is Carol?"

"I'm here, Mom," the stranger says.

"Sandi, you better deal with this woman. I think she's got a few loose screws, if you know what I mean. She's definitely two cans short of a six-pack!"

I watch as the eyes of this woman and Sandi exchange some sort of silent message. "What on earth is going on here? Do you two know each other?" I ask. "What are you up to, Sandi?"

Enough of this nonsense! I decide that I won't hang around to hear her answer.

Instead I go back to my room where I plan to start getting dressed. I remove my robe; lay it across the foot of my bed. My pretty yellow nightgown is very comfortable. I've owned it forever. I remember when my mother gave it to me as a birthday gift. I feel heaviness in my chest as I remember her funeral. It was right around the time of this birthday but more important, it was around the time of my grandson, Lucien's, birth. There are so many memories and I want to cling to them. This pretty yellow nightgown means the world to me.

Wearing my soft, silky gown I cross the room and sit down in my armchair. Thoughts of both Mom and Dad warm my heart. I remember how much my mother loved little Carol. The day she was born my mother started a trust fund for her grand-daughter. That trust fund put Carol through university. I remember it all so clearly. My memory is good! What is it with Carol and Sandi? They tell me I'm forgetful! What do they know? I remember everything. I even remember the names of my primary school teachers. I feel quiet as I sit in my chair. For just a little while I enjoy this remembering.

It was never my intention but I guess I nodded off a little because the next thing I know Carol is there shaking my arm to wake me up. She reminds me of someone else though I can't remember who that might be. "What do you want, Carol?"

"I want you to get dressed, Mom. I've come to help you. Which dress will you wear today?"

"I don't think I'll bother getting dressed today, Carol. I'm very comfortable in my pretty yellow gown. I remember when my mother gave this to me. Did you know it was on one of my birthdays?"

"Yes, Mom, I know," she sighs. "I've heard the story before. Your birthday is not far off. What do you want for your eighty-sixth?"

"Eighty-sixth? You'd never know this nightgown was that old, would you now?" I ask wondering how on earth I ever managed to soon become eighty-six years old.

"What about this soft green dress, Mom? You always liked wearing this one, didn't you?"

"It's okay. Why do I need to get dressed?"

"Didn't you say you wanted to go for a walk?"

"That's right," I remember. "It's a nice day. I want to go for a walk."

"Sandi and I are going to take you for a nice drive this morning, Mom."

"No drive! I told you I want to go for a walk!"

"We are going to drive along the lakeshore to a nice park where we can all enjoy a lovely walk, okay?"

"Bossy pants! Always have to have things your way! You always were a stubborn child, Carol!"

"Please, Mom. You look so pretty in this dress. It brings out the green in your eyes."

"It does?" Her compliment lifts my spirits. "Yes, a nice walk in a park by the lake; that's just exactly what I want to do today."

She helps me to remove my pretty yellow gown and then slips the soft green dress over my head. It slides down to cover my body and Carol ties the belt.

"Let me brush your hair for you, Mom. I know how much you like that," she says.

"I do like that very much, Carol. Thank you."

I sit back down in my armchair and watch while Carol lifts the soft brush from my dressing table. She walks around behind my chair and then with the brush she plays with my hair saying, "You have lovely hair. It's nice and soft, Mom."

I remember when I was a little girl my mother used to comb my hair and fashion it into ringlets that I never learned to appreciate. "Did you know I used to wear my hair in ringlets, Carol?"

"Yes, Mom, you told me about that before."

[270]

I'm enjoying Carol's attention and I feel disappointed when she says, "Okay, you're ready to go."

"Go?" I get up from my chair. "Where am I going, Carol? And where's my handbag? I don't want to go out without my handbag. What did you do with my handbag, Carol?"

She gives me one of those long drawn-out God-in-Heaven-help-me sighs.

"It's right there on your bed, Mom," she says as she passes it to me. I accept my handbag which I carry over my arm. "Thank you, Carol." Taking my other arm she walks with me out of the apartment, along the hallway to the elevator.

It's a beautiful, bright summer day. Outside the apartment building we follow the cement walk-way and soon reach the roadside where I see Sandi sitting behind the wheel of her car. "Are you going to work now, Sandi?" Not waiting for an answer I tell her, "Carol and I are going for a walk in the park now."

"Yes, I know," she says. "I'm going to drive you both to the park. Get in the car, Mom."

"Oh, okay. That's very kind of you, Sandi."

Carol opens the car door wide. "You get into the back seat with me."

"You don't need to be so bossy, Carol!"

To Sandi I say, "Don't drive too fast. Remember! I don't like driving fast!"

It is a very good day for a drive. Sandi doesn't drive too fast and I feel very happy because in what seems like no time at all we have reached the lake.

I see the lovely blue water of Lake Ontario as we drive along the lakeshore. We pass the boardwalk in the Beaches and I remember when I walked there with my boyfriend long ago. I remember the day I married my boyfriend. I walked with him and pushed Carol in her pram along that boardwalk. His name was Jerry. I remember those walks.

"Driver, stop the car!" I shout.

The car keeps moving. "Carol, tell the driver to stop this car at once!"

"Mom," Carol says, "we don't want to stop. We are going to the park for a nice walk, remember?"

"I don't want to go to a park. I want to walk on the boardwalk! If you won't make the driver stop, I'll stop her myself." I swing my handbag and whack her a good one on the back of her head.

"Ow!" the taxi driver cries.

"Mom, stop it!" Carol yells as she yanks the handbag out of my hands.

"Give me back my purse!"

[272]

"I will, Mom, when we get to the park."

Soon the taxi pulls off the road. I see we are on a very long driveway and soon I can see a very large house; so big I think it must be a hotel. The driver keeps going past the hotel and carries on down the road until she comes to a park. I can see the water now. The lake is very calm. This is a very nice place to go for a walk.

The driver stops the car and opens the back door to assist me as I get out. I'm surprised to see the driver is Sandi. "Thank you, Sandi," I say. "I didn't know you were going to walk with us today. I must say this is very pleasant."

There is a lovely path along the water's edge. I slip my arm through Carol's and together we begin our walk. Sandi walks on my other side. I don't take her arm because I need to carry my handbag.

"What's the name of that big hotel we passed?"

"I'm not sure," Sandi responds.

"I don't know, Mom," Carol answers.

"Let's walk up that way," Sandi suggests. "We can go inside for a nice cup of tea. Would you like that, Mom?"

I would and I tell her so.

[273]

As we draw closer to the hotel I can see the sign over the main door. It says *Hawkwind Retirement Home.*

I'm on to them. Right away I think of Jason Knobest. "You tricked me! You lied to me!"

"No, Mom," Sandi says. "Why all the fuss? We're just visiting. We are going in for a cup of tea. Didn't you say you wanted a cup of tea, Mom?"

"Yes, I did, didn't I?"

"It's okay, Mom," Carol says. "You will like it here. This is a nice place."

"How nice, Carol? Maybe I'm not dressed classy enough. I'm just wearing my old walking shoes."

"Mom, you are so pretty in your soft green dress. No one is going to pay any attention or notice your shoes."

"Well, if you're sure."

"I'm sure," she smiles.

Inside the hotel I take a good look around. There are round tables with armchairs and there are a couple of sofas. I even see some lawn chairs through the glass doors that lead out to a deck. I have to admit it is a very nice place. "But Carol, how come all the hotel guests are so old? I feel like I'm in a mausoleum!"

We sit at a table. We wait for a waitress. We wait a long time. I look around at all the bald heads and the gaping mouths on the sleeping old women. What kind of a hotel is this?

The waitress arrives but I notice she looks more like a nurse than a waitress. "What on earth is going on here?" I ask but no one takes the time to answer.

I see Sandi whisper something to the hospital waitress and she goes away.

Again we wait. "Service is slow," I say.

The sun's rays through the glass deck doors feel good but make me sleepy. Yes, I am feeling very drowsy.

Then, "Wake up, Mom," I hear Carol yelling.

I open my eyes to see a young woman wearing light blue scrubs. She places the steaming mug on the table in front of me. "Here's a nice cup of tea for you, Ellen."

"Thank you," I answer. "But this tea is in a mug. Don't you know that tea should be served hot in a china cup with a saucer?"

The waitress just stands there like a dummy. She doesn't say a word. No, she just stands there and stares at me.

"You don't have to look at me like that," I say. "I do know what I'm talking about. Mugs are for coffee. Tea should always be served in a cup!" Then, I ask Carol and Sandi, "Aren't you having tea?"

"No, Mom," they say.

"Well, I can't say as I blame you. What kind of a hotel is this that serves tea in a mug? Wouldn't you think they would know tea should always be served in a cup with a saucer?"

"It's okay, Mom. Don't worry about it. You drink your tea and then we'll do a wander around the hotel," Sandi says.

"Would you like that?" asks Carol.

"No, I want to walk outside by the water."

"We'll do that after we check out the hotel, Mom," Sandi says.

"Bossy pants! You're as bad as your sister! Always have to do things your way!"

I finish drinking my tea. We leave the dining room and I walk around the hotel with them.

"Nice place, eh, Mom?"

The next thing I know Sandi opens a door and leads me into one of the hotel rooms. I see a bed by the window. I see an armchair not much different from the one I have at home in my bedroom. It's even the same colour. I see a bookshelf and as I run my finger along the backs of the books I think it's odd that the shelf holds some of the very books I own. Then I notice a couple of photos. How very odd! I see a photo of a bride and groom. When I look closely I see that the bride is me. And my Jerry was so very young in that wedding picture. I see another photo of Carol and Sandi atop a dresser. This is very strange. I'm confused. I pinch my arm to see if I'm awake.

I decide to open one of the drawers in the dresser. In the top drawer I see my pretty yellow nightgown; the very one my mother gave to me on my birthday; the very gown I was wearing just this morning. At least I think it was just this morning; I'm a little confused.

I turn around to look at Carol and Sandi. I see the waitress is still wearing the medical scrubs. I am wondering why she is also there in the room with us. "What's going on, Carol?

"Everything is okay. There is nothing going on, Mom."

"But where are we, Sandi?"

"Why, we are in your room, Mom," Sandi replies.

"In my room?"

I move to the window. Looking through the windowpane I see the lovely park. I see the blue water and the path that runs along beside the lake.

"I want to go for a walk."

"Sure, Mom," Carol says. I see Sandi look at the waitress. She smiles and nods.

Why should I need her approval to go for a walk; or for anything at all for that matter? "Who are you?" I ask her.

"I'm Susan," she says.

"Oh," I say. I don't remember her but I don't need to let them know I've forgotten something again. "Are you coming for a walk with us?"

"Sure," she says.

The walk along the path by the lake is pleasurable and invigorating. The skies are bluer than blue and my feet follow the concrete path. But after a while I begin to feel a little tired and decide to let the others in on it. "I'm growing a little weary," I say.

"We'll turn back now," Sandi says.

"Ready to go back to your room, Mom?" Carol asks.

"Yes, I think so. Maybe I'll take a little nap."

"Good idea," Sandi says.

Back in my room I sit on the edge of my bed. I run my hand over the silky softness of the colourful, floral bedspread. I look at Carol, Sandi and Susan. "I want to take a little nap now, girls. Why are you all hanging about in my room? Don't you have anything better to do?"

"Mom, do you have everything you need? Is there anything you would like me to bring when we come to visit you?"

"Come to visit me? Carol, what on earth are you talking about?"

"Nothing, Mom. You just rest."

I recline on my bed. As I move my hands back and forth on the familiar slippery silk of my bedspread I allow my gaze to travel to the photos on my dresser; the books on my shelf. I feel confused. I am puzzled. Everything looks the same yet somehow it all seems different. I move my gaze to the window. Getting up from my bed I walk to the window and looking out I see the blue water once again. Funny, but I don't remember having a lake outside my bedroom window. How on earth could I forget something like that?

"Carol, there's a lake outside my window."

"Yes, Mom," she says.

"Sandi, I don't see my bench. And where is my Hummingtree?"

She didn't answer me; nobody answered me. "Why not come back to bed and have a little nap, Mom?

Deep down in my heart of hearts I am wondering and I am worrying. Where am I? Where is my Hummingtree? Where is my treasured yellow quartz rock? Has God forsaken me altogether?

But I answer, "Yes, I think I'll do that."

"Good," Carol says. "It's past your nap time."

Nap time. I remember when I'm a little girl and my mother tells me it's nap time. I look around for my mother but she's not in the room. I see Carol. I see another woman who looks familiar. Her name is on the tip of my tongue but I can't recall it. There's another person there and by the way she's dressed she should be in a hospital; not here in my room. Who are these people?

"We're leaving now but we will see you soon," the familiar one says. "Is there anything you need?"

I'm very sleepy; too tired to wait for Mommy to come tuck me in. To the strange people I don't know what to say. Do I need anything? I'm having some difficulty remembering who I am. I can't think of anything I need. To satisfy them and to get them out of my room I say, "There is one thing I need. Sometimes I forget so I need you to remember me. Will you do that for me?"

"Always," one person answers.

The waitress in scrubs just smiles but the other woman is crying. I wonder why she is crying. Doesn't she want to go home?

They close my door behind them. I was beginning to think they would never leave. I would like to go out into my backyard. I would like to sit beneath my Lilac and talk to God through my yellow quartz rock. I want to do this but perhaps I will need to wait and do it tomorrow. Yes, that's what I will do in the morning. Surely the Good Lord will understand.

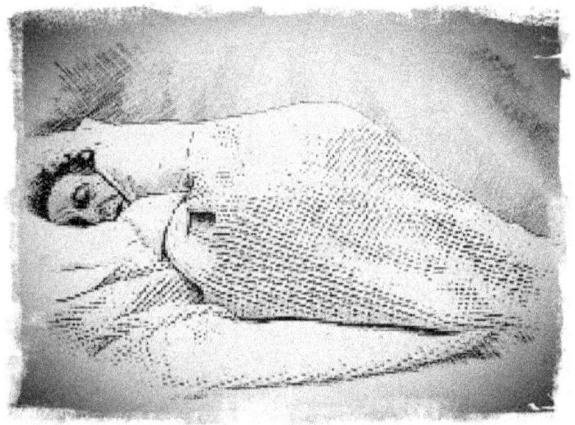

He always does. I am very weary now. I roll over onto my side and welcome sleep.

SEVENTEEN

SEVENTEEN:

Time To Go Home:

I don't know what to do. I don't know what is expected of me. I'm not sure where I am and I don't think I like it here. Just like a rain shower on a sunny day I don't know whether to smile or to cry. I'm quite comfortable actually as I lay here snuggled in my blanket.

When I open my tired eyes I can see barely yellow walls wrapped around my bed and now I can see that this is a hospital bed. I allow my eyes to wander and now I can see three other beds just like the one I'm in. Yes, I am in a hospital. Why am I in a hospital? Am I ill?

Inside the other beds I see old, yellowy white heads poking out above the beige blankets. I don't like what I see. I decide I don't want to see it anymore. I close my eyes and try to go to sleep.

When I open my eyes again confusion reigns. One moment I see the heads peeking out from blankets on what I am sure are the hospital beds and in the next moment the hospital room disappears. In its place I see nothing but a huge solitary white carnation bobbing up and down in the midst of a field of wheat sheaves that are waving in the wind. Very strange indeed. I wonder if I should wave back at them.

My mouth starts to salivate. The white carnation is gone now. I know I am back in the hospital room when a nurse arrives at my bedside and wipes the slippery wetness from my mouth's folded corners as she repeats, "Sit up, Ellen."

She doesn't need to keep repeating herself. After all, I heard her the first time.

I feel the warmth of the sun and I will myself to lift my head from this tired pillow. I am not trying to be difficult. I do want to sit up. I want to sit up, not to please the nurse but to capture some sense of aliveness within me. But the force of the rain keeps me pinned where I hover above the abyss of insanity.

Where is all the rain coming from and how is it possible I am not getting wet? And how is it that I feel the heat from the sun that is blazing overhead? That is the sun, isn't it? Surely it's not just a large light fixture up in the ceiling.

I would like to ask the nurse but for some reason my mouth is sealed shut. I doubt the nurse would hear me anyway. She is too busy talking; saying the same thing over and over again until I want to tell her to be quiet once and for all. "Sit up, Ellen!" she insists.

How did I ever land myself in such a predicament? I swear I did not mean to outlive myself. I had often told my daughters that it was the last thing I wanted to do. "I don't want to out-live myself," I often said once I passed my seventieth birthday. Yet here I am. Too much in life has not gone according to my plan. Now I am old and there is no one to care that such a plan ever existed.

I want to tell the nurse that I want to go home. I want to tell her I am not just another old yellowy empty head. I want to tell her that I still have lots of life in me. But I feel my eyes closing. I want to keep them open but sometimes my eyes have a mind of their own. They are stubborn eyes.

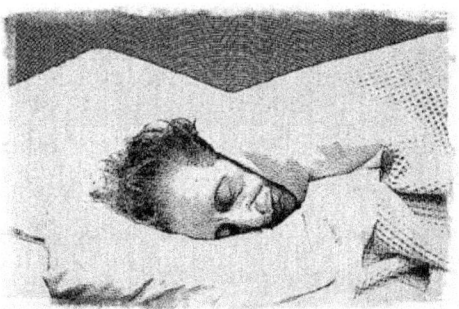

I let them have their way but not for long. I open my eyes again and at last I am able to open my mouth to speak my truth but the nurse has gone. In her place my daughters, Carol and Sandi, are standing at my bedside. They are tearful.

"What's wrong, girls? Why are you crying? Is Lucien okay? Where is my little grandson?"

But my daughters don't hear me. My voice got lost. It must have followed the nurse out of the room. My girls are met by a stupid old mother whose mouth drips nothing but saliva which forms little lakes in the folds of her mouth.

"I want to go home, Carol. Sandi, please take me home. I don't want to stay here. Please don't leave me here." My words flow into the water and sink into oblivion.

I'm begging but now my daughters turn their backs on me. They are leaving the room. No, no, I am mistaken. Thank God, they are not leaving yet. They are greeting someone else who is entering the room. Who is it? Who is that man with them?

"Good afternoon, Mrs. Dawson."

Now I recognize him. I know who he is. If only I could move my tired body I would surely turn my back on him. That is what I want to do. Yes, now I know who he is. I remember you, Mr. Jason Knobest. Always pretending to be nice but I know all you want is to take me back to that Hawkwind Retirement Home.

"Girls, don't listen to him. Listen to me, Carol. I beg of you, Sandi, do not take me back to Hawkwind. I want to be in my own home. Please just take me home. Please! *Dear God in heaven, please give me back my voice.*"

But God has also turned his back on this old woman. He will not give my words wings that they might fly to the ears of someone, anyone, who will hear my plea.

Carol and Sandi are talking in very low tones now with Jason Knobest. I want to hear what is being said but I can feel myself travelling now. I feel myself leaving this dreadful place filled with old people in hospital beds.

Oh, thank you, God, for hearing my plea. Thank you for bringing me home.

Now I am walking into my backyard and I see a very deep hole in the ground. It is not much more than a foot or two wide. What is this? The hole can't be for my grave. I'm fatter than that.

Then a loud and distinct ticking sound comes up from the depths of the hole. Now I remember. "I know who you are. I met you here once before. Are you here to warn me of my impending death? Back off Banshee!"

And then, just like that, I am back in the hospital and I hear that Knobest fellow again.

"Mrs. Dawson, when you are ready to leave the hospital your cozy room still awaits you in the Hawkwind Retirement Home."

I want to tell him to piss off and leave an old woman alone. I want to tell my daughters I don't belong here in the hospital. And I don't belong in a retirement home. I want to be where I belong. I want to be back in my own home. But no matter how hard I try I cannot convince the words to pass my lips and be heard.

"She can't hear you," I hear Carol say.

"You don't know what she can hear," Sandi cried.

"Your mother hears you, Sandi! Don't send me back to Hawkwind. I want to go home."

"Don't be a fool, Sandi. It's wishful thinking on your part. For all intents and purposes Mom is gone. The best thing for us to do is to accept the truth of the matter."

"I'm not gone, Carol. *God in Heaven, why don't you tell them I'm still here?*

I feel the softness of Carol's kiss on my forehead. I'm warmed by Sandi's touch as she holds my hand. "I'll come back this evening," she promises.

"Lucien is coming by later this afternoon to visit with you, Mom," Carol says. "And I will be back to see you tomorrow morning. I love you."

"Love you, Mom," Sandi says.

"I love you both!" I'm shouting but nothing but water wets the air. "You were my life. You girls and Lucien were my only reason for living! Please don't leave."

But they are gone.

I'm abandoned in this hospital. I'm all alone now in this godforsaken hospital bed.

But then, no - no, I'm not alone. There is someone here in the room with me. I feel a presence. *Dad, is that you? How can it be you? Am I dead now, God? Daddy, am I dead?*

"I'm sorry I left you when you were so very young, Ellen."

My father is apologizing to me. How is this possible? I cannot answer my own question but I do know he is here beside my bed and he is giving me his best explanation. I am surprised to see that he is young and he is very handsome. How is it possible that my father is younger than me? Again I cannot answer my own question. Yet I cannot deny the truth of the vision appearing before my very own eyes. My father is here and he is talking to me.

"I listened to the call of the wild and that is what took me away from you and your mother, Ellen. Just before I left this earth and journeyed to my heavenly home I bequeathed to you the yellow quartz rock. With this rock there will always be a Hummingtree and this Hummingtree will be with you for as long as you live on God's good earth."

"Daddy, the Hummingtree has been my saving grace. God has always listened and talked to me through the magical rock. But look around you and you will see for yourself that there is no rock here in this hated hospital. There's no Hummingtree. I very much want to go home now. Daddy, are you here to take me home? Please say you have come here to take me back home?"

"Not just yet, Ellen. The reason I am here is because I've come to talk to you about the yellow quartz rock."

"I thought it would always be with me, Daddy, but I've searched and I can't find it anywhere in this awful place."

"Soon you will be coming home with me, Ellen. I want to talk to you about the legacy of the rock. You will have no further need of it once you go home to live with your heavenly Father. It is important that you decide now who will receive the gifts of the yellow quartz rock beneath the Hummingtree."

"Without question, we know who will inherit my legacy, Daddy."

"Is it Sandi? Carol?"

"No, Daddy. There is no doubt in my mind that my Sandi has enough compassion to carry her through any situation life decides to throw at her. And as for Carol, she always has her feet on the ground; stable and sensible. I know she will have the inner strength to carry on without me. And my daughters are never alone. I thank God that they have each other."

"If not my grand-daughters, then who will be the beneficiary, Ellen?"

"Why, Lucien, of course. Who else but Lucien would receive these gifts of prophecy?"

"It is decided?"

"Yes, Daddy."

"Then it is finished. I must go now. Your mother is waiting for me."

"I miss Mommy and I love you, Daddy. Do you have to go so soon?"

"Yes."

"Am I dying, Daddy?"

"Ellen, don't ask such a question of your father!"

Now I am bathed in the warmth of His heavenly light. **"Oh, God, I'm so happy to see you. I thought you had forsaken me."**

"Know I am with you always, Ellen. Are you so foolish to think I cannot speak to you without the aid of a yellow quartz rock or the crutch of a Hummingtree?"

"Yes, too often I have been too foolish."

"Never forget, Ellen. It will rain when I say it rains and the sun will shine when I say. When I decide it is time, you will go home and not one second before or after. Only I decide when it is time for you to go home."

"Daddy was just here, Lord. Will my mother or my father be your messenger? Or will it be Marielle?"

"Here you are, more than ninety years old and are you telling me that you still want to traipse after your cousin, Marielle?"

[292]

"I have never stopped missing her and, dear God, I have never stopped loving her."

"And that is as it should be, Ellen. I tell you now that your parents and your cousin; even that hapless husband of yours, have all made their journey home."

"Jerry's promise to me was deathless. He assured me of his undying love. Then he took off and left me alone to raise my girls when the job was only half finished."

"He kept his promise, Ellen. I urge you to look at it this say. If Jerry had not left you, would you have met William, the carpenter, or Jethro who loved you?"

"In all these years, I never thought of it that way, Lord."

"That just goes to prove you are not quite ready to go home yet. Sometimes even I wonder if you will ever learn that everything that happens on this earth happens for a reason."

"Forgive me, Lord. I'm a foolish old woman."

"Yes, you have been a difficult child at times, Ellen, but I love all my children. That includes you. Now say good-bye to your father. And don't ask him such a question. Remember, I decide the hour of your departure."

"Yes, Lord." I feel healing warmth on my cheek. "Oh, Daddy, I thought you had left but you are still here with me."

"Yes, but only for a moment. Know that when you return to your heavenly home the yellow quartz rock will plant itself in the earth near to Lucien no matter where in the world he chooses to be. The rock will always find its home beneath a Hummingtree, be it an Oak, a Maple, or ....."

"Or a Lilac, Daddy?"

"Yes, Ellen, maybe even a Lilac."

I felt bathed in the warmth of my Daddy's smile. I felt comforted. I felt safe. I felt loved. Again my eyes decided to close.

I guess I fell asleep then because when I woke up the nurse was there again. She was fumbling about with the intravenous. I want to tell her that filling me up with all that old sugar water is not going to sweeten me up. Nothing is going to make me like it here. Funny how I can't get the words out to talk to people who are alive but I have no trouble at all talking to those who have already gone to their reward. I don't know how I am able to talk to dead people. It must be something they're putting in all that old sugar water!

I open my eyes. Suddenly I feel snuggly warm beneath a blanket of happiness. He is a sight for sore eyes. Surely now the stuck corners of my sloppy mouth have transformed into a smile.

"Lucien, I'm thrilled to see you. I've been talking with the Lord and with your grandfather, Leon. I'm assured that the yellow quartz rock and my Hummingtree will always be with you."

"How is my Gram doing, nurse?" I hear Lucien ask. He didn't hear a word I said. My words refuse to leave my heart.

I glare at the nurse as she gives her head a few negative shakes.

I continue to glare at her but she pays little attention. I want to stick my tongue out at her. What a nasty woman she is shaking her head in such a depressing manner and upsetting my Lucien. What does she know? Only God knows.

Then my ears are soothed by the soft sound of Lucien's voice. "I don't know if you can hear me or not, Gram, but I want you to know that I will still visit you once they move you back into the Hawkwind Retirement Home."

"No, Lucien. No, my child. Surely you cannot believe they are going to move me back into that place. I want to go home, Lucien."

"I have to go, Gram. I'm truly sorry my visit is short. I give you my word I will stay longer next time. I don't know if you realize it, Gram, but you were my rock throughout a challenging childhood. You rescued me from that tree where the bullies tied me when I was a young lad. And remember the day that doomed helicopter crashed in the woods behind the house?"

"I remember, Lucien. I remember you called it a hella chopper!"

"You spread your body over mine on the road to protect me. That is something I will never forget. That is a memory I will treasure forever. Gram, I don't need to tell you that I've always had learning difficulties, and I guess I always will, but you were the one who taught me that whatever I believed I could achieve. When I most needed your love, you lived for me. You carried me when I couldn't take the steps on my own."

"Please take me home with you, Lucien," I begged.

I feel his tears on my face as he kisses me good-bye.

"Why are you crying, Lucien?"

He doesn't hear me.

I'm falling asleep but I wake up again when I'm surprised and shocked to hear guitar music. I open my eyes. There he is; Jethro Tunkel, my dearest friend and loving partner. His crooked smile shines through his shaggy, white beard. Short, round and glowing; Jethro, who never intended to outstay his welcome, was a part of my life for many years before he went to his reward. Jethro is playing his guitar and, yes, he is singing.

[296]

"Did you say goodbye, were you in love, did you have faith in God up above? Looking for faith, searching for hope, searching for that something that helps us to cope."

His voice is as clear as an angel's. Hello Jethro, my friend. My, how the neighbours loved to gossip about us. And we finally did give them something to talk about didn't we, my love?

"That we did, Ellen. Do you remember this old song called Beautiful World? It was written by that fellow who shares my surname."

"Yes, I remember Bruce Tunkel and I remember the song. Jethro, you can hear me?"

"Of course I hear you, Ellen."

"Am I dead yet, Jethro?"

"No, not yet. The word is you will be going home soon."

"I want to go home, Jethro. I want to sit on the bench beneath my Lilac tree. I want to feel the healing vibrations and listen to God once more."

"Soon Ellen." And then he was singing again. *'Did you say good-bye? Were you in love? Did you have faith in God up above?"*

"Yes, to all your questions, Jethro. It was not easy to say good-bye to you. I love you still. And my faith in God sustains me even today."

[297]

"That's my girl, Ellen!"

Memories flood my mind. He's my Jethro from the Hebrew 'Yitro' meaning abundance. When I thought I was going to lose my house, along came Jethro with his never-ending songs and quotations. With Jethro by my side I did not need a lottery win. With him my cup overflowed with peace, health and prosperity.

"Good-bye, sweet Ellen. I'll see you soon again."

Jethro is gone too soon and now I see no one but the nurse. She's talking about me behind my back to somebody I can't see. Throughout my life many people have made it their business to talk about me. I always pretended that I didn't care. I acted as though I let it all fall like water off a duck's back but inside it hurt when people said mean things about me. Just because I talked to my God in a rock; just because my church was a bench beneath my Hummingtree; just because I dared to be a Daniel and do things different from the way most folks do things; people said mean things about me. Yes, they did.

Who is the nurse talking to? What is she saying anyway? I want to know and I wish they would come closer so that I could hear them. They should all remember I'm ninety years old and my hearing isn't what it used to be.

Then out of nowhere, or so it seems, a voice shouts. All of a sudden my room is crowded. I can see all the people right there in front of me in my hospital room. They are all milling about and listening to something. What do they hear? Everyone is listening.

With me in the room is Mom, Daddy, Carol and Sandi; Jerry, William, and even my old neighbour, Emma. I see Reverend Wilson from the Methodist church. I can see Jethro and my boy, Lucien. Even Gregory Hamilton is there still carrying an apology in his quiet demeanor. I had never forgotten but I had forgiven Gregory long ago. I see everyone I loved and as my eyes receive the blessing of their presence I feel the warm wetness of my beautiful Kris's loving lick on my hand; our beautiful German Shepherd who was there with Jethro on his last day. Yes, I see everyone I loved. I see everyone who helped to shape my life.

There in that hospital room I see all the people bow their heads and I know that they listen to every sound the voice makes. I listen too. How could I not listen to such loud shouting? I'm not scared but I can see my loved ones are frightened. They cringe as though in fear.

The voice shouts again. Then I know it is the voice of God. In all the years I communed with my Lord, He had never shouted in my presence before. His voice had always been the voice of reason; the voice of hope; the quiet voice within.

But not this day. This day the Lord is shouting.

"Thomas, set up the stairway!"

I wonder, "Who on earth is Thomas?"

And God, as always, is there for me. He stops issuing orders to Thomas and takes the time to reassure me. Yesterday, today, and always, my God is a loving God.

What a pleasure it is to look up into the face of glory that is my Lord and Saviour and to know that He is there for me alone.

"Thomas is not of the earth, Ellen. You still have much to learn. Don't worry. Thomas knows what to do. It's time to go home now, Ellen."

"Oh, good! Thank you, God. I've been begging everyone to let me go home. No one but you has heard me."

"Take my hand. They will miss you but be assured you will meet everyone again. It's time to ascend. Are you ready to go home, Ellen?"

"Yes, Lord, I'm ready."

EIGHTEEN

EIGHTEEN:

Summing it up - A narrative poem:

The Hummingtree

*The tree bowed down his branches and spoke
aloud to me,*

*He said, "Dear child, you won't believe the
things that I can see."*

*I listened from my garden bench and prayed
for disabuse*

*For many years some folks have said I've more
than one screw loose.*

*I feel the warmth of God's kind sun, though high
above indeed,*

To measure its true path on high

a sextant I would need.

Ellen and The Hummingtree

I hear the sound of Hummingtree, it echoes through

the years,

The voice of God speaks through my rock and wipes

away my tears.

The voice begins in yellow quartz and rises more or

less

Vibrating through my Hummingtree then gifts me

with largess.

It all began when Daddy died and I was just a child,

Father willed to me the journal he penned north while

in the wild.

In the basement of my mother's home 'neath plastic it

was hidden,

When I found Dad's diary in the wall, I read and did

as bidden.

The journal, it was strangely wrapped inside an old,

strange skin.

Its value was immeasurable, to me, his next of kin...

Just fifteen when I found the book but for years I'd

heard the legend,

The journal was beneath a rock is what I'd heard

folks mention.

My auntie said the book was cursed and said Dad's

boots were haunted,

The journal was all I had of one who had made me feel unwanted.

My mother was a genteel soul much loved by friends and family,

That father's tastes were plebeian was Reverend Wilson's homily.

My Hummingtree enfolds me within her sheltering arms

She shows me all the things she's seen and keeps me free from harm.

She softly said, "You'll not believe all that I have viewed,"

"But I do believe," I answer, unsure, with voice subdued.

"I do believe because I've seen visions, sights amazing,

As I've talked to God within my rock while on garden

bench I'm lazing."

"Your faith is strong and will endure", God, through

yellow quartz declares.

'Tis true, dear God, and strong it stays. I've even lost

my fear of bears"

I'm sure I heard God chuckle, He remembered that

hot day

When bear stole mother's figurine while in my yard

he played.

That's but one of many memories my God and I have

shared,

I've sat on earth beneath my tree, to Him my soul I've

bared.

My Hummingtree was once a Birch, indeed, 'twas

once an Oak,

Today it is a Lilac tree, 'tis truth I speak; no joke.

Today I'm growing old and tired but I do still recall

The day my father's journal at last explained it all.

I was but five when he took off. I felt alone,

abandoned.

Mother told me, "Ellen dear, freedom makes him

gladdened."

What did I care for her defense of actions

disappointing?

As little child without a Dad I watched the fingers

pointing.

Some said Dad's boots were haunted and they said

that of his knife,

But my mother, she said nothing and she was daddy's

wife.

Aunt said knife was under curse, sharp but can't cut

butter.

Did Mom agree? I'll never know; not one word would

she utter.

'Twas Mom who hid the journal, she thought she'd

hid it well.

I found the book; 'twas mine to find as rock 'neath

Hummingtree did tell.

My father's name was Leon and James Bay was his

home,

From the time that he was twenty he preferred to be

alone.

He traded with the James Bay Cree, he traded furs for

food

Powerful spirit Manitou he believed and understood.

Away up north where wild winds howl Daddy's feet

stayed warm,

Inside those boots the Cree did make they weathered

every storm.

Dad's notes inside his journal about the boots he wore

Explained the curse or blessing; intention declared

score.

And since Dad's purpose was sincere he deemed the

boots good fortune,

He walked in faith, alive and pure, and followed

spiritual doctrine.

Dad's knife was honed on yellow quartz by his friend

who was a Cree,

He taught Great Spirit's wisdom beneath the

Tamarack tree.

The ancient being called Great Spirit was my father's

teacher,

He taught compassion, hope and love for every living

creature.

Great Spirit's voice came from the rock that sat

beneath tall pine

And promised that upon Dad's death the quartz rock

would be mine.

My child tears fell on daddy's hand. I begged him,

"Please don't go."

[311]

That day he left me long ago, he was Warrior of

Rainbow.

Yearning for the wilderness Daddy left the city,

He left my Mom and me alone. My aunt said 'twas a

pity.

Great Spirit's promise to my Dad was God to me

would speak

Through the rock, beneath the tree, when answered

prayer I'd seek.

The word of Ancient of the Ancients was to me the

rock be left,

Because a child whose father dies feels lost, alone,

bereft.

This miracle it did occur, yellow quartz my God

provided,

Since my Daddy left this earth 'neath Hummingtree

I've abided.

As my father did before me, I sit beneath the tree that

hums,

And listen to the voice of Spirit through the rock that

overcomes.

I also sit on God's good earth and hear sound that

fills the branches,

This hum's great gift is inner peace and wisdom that

enhances.

Warrior of Rainbow was my dad. How can I be less?

Through his journal he is close to me in spirit, I

confess.

Leon Campbell was his name, he taught me of Great

Spirit's ways,

Ellen and The Hummingtree

He taught me joy in solitude, his love for me in my

heart stays.

These things took place when I was a kid, a long time

ago that was,

I asked the tree, "Did Daddy love me?" Tree

answered, "He did and still does."

When I grew up I met a man, one by the name of

Jerry,

I thought he loved me, and perhaps he did, so this

young man I did marry.

It happened one night there was a storm, the winds

blew hard and the roof did leak,

The Oak tree cried and bore my grief, from that night

onward Jerry would not speak.

Like Mommy before me I was alone; Jerry left me two

children to raise,

Burden or blessing, to God I give praise, but the sins

of the fathers have haunted my days.

Just like my father, he went far away even though he

had promised undying love,

My children, abandoned, filled with despair. Dad

wasn't there when push came to shove.

My daughters' lives flourished, of them I felt proud,

My fears I kept silent, I did not speak aloud

Like my mother before me I said not a word

About the kids'' father by that woman lured.

I needed a confidante, needed a friend; I needed

someone to listen,

To hear my worries and lighten my load, to comfort

when only tears glisten.

On days such as those I would go to backyard; I would

sit on the bench near my rock,

I would hear the tree's hum and feel not so alone,

close weary eyes while to God I would talk.

And God always showed me His might and His power;

He taught me I'm never unaided,

Whatever the problem He listened with love, I was

washed in His words which cascaded.

My two lovely daughters, Sandi and Carol, grew up

and lived lives of their own,

I missed my dear children but not a day passed when

they didn't visit or phone.

Then Carol did marry and she bore a son; Lucien was

his name, my first grandson,

When Lucien was little his Dad disappeared; another

abandonment, what could be done?

While Carol did work, Lucien stayed with me; a

burden he carried, he was slow in the head,

I did all to protect him, to keep my boy safe, but others

did taunt him, he cried in his bed.

I always kept watch when he came home from school

to be sure he travelled in safety,

But one day I faltered, my boy was in peril, their

torture was cruel, fierce and lengthy.

My heart was heavy and drowning in sorrow, I could

not find my Lucien, my boy.

I sat 'neath my tree and I prayed blessed be, bring him

home, this small child, my heart's joy.

I sat 'neath my tree and prayed please God, help me.

To my ear from the rock came direction,

Through the woods I did run shouting Lucien, my

son! God offered my grandson protection.

[318]

Tied to a tree they had left him to suffer naked and

laden with grief,

I brought the boy home; comfort I gave him;

Hummingtree's guidance strengthened belief.

This is but one of my many great memories of times

'neath my dear Hummingtree

Now Lucien is grown, a fine upstanding man, who

visits his Gram no matter how busy.

I've been single for years but I did have my chances,

Ellen and The Hummingtree

William entered my life and he took me to dances.

He was the carpenter who made great discovery

Of roots from a tree causing swift recovery,

And from these old roots upon which he had stumbled

he created a fine masterpiece,

Which he offered to me as a gift I still treasure,

forever its value will always increase.

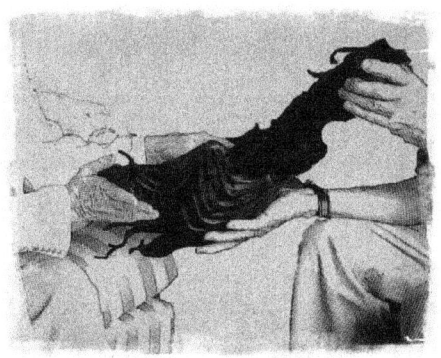

I accepted his gift and twelve short years later William

asked me to be his life partner.

I sat 'neath my tree, sought God's will for my life;

with regret I declined this man's ardor.

More years passed by and my carpenter died,

I will miss him, I sighed. On my bench I cried.

Living alone, growing old, feeling useless, I often

would sit 'neath my tree while I prayed,

I communed with my Lord, I spoke with emotion,

townsfolk all thought I was crazed.

Both daughters, well-meaning, trying to be dutiful

decided I needed to move from my house.

They thought it was time I took residence elsewhere

with other old folks also lacking a spouse.

Along came this fellow, the name Jason Knobest, who

tried to convince me I needed to move,

I wasted no time showing him to the door and let my

kids know, "Yes, I do disapprove!"

Ellen and The Hummingtree

I remained quite alone and soon grew much older;

finances were giving me strife,

Jethro Tunkel arrived and he turned things around by

singing and playing his life.

While I sat 'neath my tree Jethro sang songs to me,

words of spiritual love, faith and hope,

He became my best friend; he lifted me up when I

thought I had reached the end of my rope.

Much older than me, Jethro shared his great wisdom,

With bright, crooked smile, shining through shaggy

beard,

He sang songs about waiting and reasons for such,

Desperation was gone once Jethro appeared.

Through Jethro I learned that my life is a song,

I learned that it's in my own home I belong.

From Kris we promised we never would part

From the beautiful Shepherd who stole my heart,

I think of my cousin, the dear Marielle,

Ellen and The Hummingtree

Behind her I always would follow

Then when we grew older and baked that meat pie

Filled with whiskey that she made me swallow

She wasn't aware that when she wasn't there I shared

love with George and we'd play

That secret, well kept, shared with my God alone,

remains in my heart to this day

Then the laptop appeared and along came Gregory

At the time he was hurtful but today just a memory.

I've known joy and sorrow and so it shall be;

I am old but I'm woman desiring no pity.

I've enjoyed reminiscing; it's a joy to remember, the

people, the good times and bad,

I sit 'neath my Hummingtree warmed by my rock I

thank God for family and friends I've had.

[324]

But it's not over yet, though I'm old and I'm gray,

I've still time ahead not to be wasted,

Mighty Hummingtree bows as I bow to my Lord and

give thanks for the good life I've tasted.

Mighty branches bow down and the leaves touch the

ground,

When the wind shouts and makes me seek cover,

I stand strong like my rock; I can bend like my tree,

I've grown old knowing God is my anchor.

__About the author:__

Audrey Austin has written novels, novellas, poetry, plays, anthologies and short stories which dare to stand alone. Her joy is creative writing.

Learn more by visiting Austin's author page at http://www.amazon.com/author/audreyaustin

http://www.facebook.com/audreyaustinca

her blog at http://writecreatively.blogspot.com

About the Illustrator:

Susan Ruby Krupp; http://yuneekpix.com

Living and freelancing in Elliot Lake, Susan has developed what she affectionately calls "Phollage". It's a combination of photography, painting and digital manipulation that she has explored and developed using tools of the computer. The possibilities are virtually endless, and she's intrigued that the learning curve continues to take her on this fantastic journey. She specializes in portraiture (both people and pets) as well as more mainstream graphic design.

<u>BOOKS BY AUDREY AUSTIN</u>

Sara, a Canadian Saga

Reawakening

The Silent Star Plus a Dozen

Keeping It Simple

Ellen and The Hummingtree

Moose Road – a Canadian Tragedy

Beyond The Blue

Recompense

When God Gives Us Spring

Social Studies – a Trilogy – Books 1, 2 and 3

www.ingramcontent.com/pod-product-compliance
Lightning Source LLC
Chambersburg PA
CBHW072058020726
47501CB00003B/627